The Diary of a Madman

Selected Novels of Lu Xun

ISBN: 9798397586405
Imprint: Daybreak Studios

CONTENTS

The Diary of a Madman 1

Kong Yiji 13

Blessing 18

Tomorrow 36

The Story of Hair 43

At the Restaurant 48

Soap 60

Dragon Boat Festival 71

The Sky Mender 80

Shattered Departure: A Fragmented Memoir 90

To the Moon 109

White Light 121

Brothers 127

THE DIARY OF A MADMAN

A certain individual, whose name is now concealed, were all my good friends back when we were in school. After being separated for many years, the news gradually ceased. Recently, I happened to hear about a serious illness that befell one of them. As I returned to my hometown, I took a detour to visit, only to meet one person who turned out to be the brother of the person suffering from the illness. I apologized for the long journey to visit, but it turned out that the illness had already been cured, and they had left to await an appointment in a certain place. I laughed heartily and showed them two volumes of a diary, claiming that it revealed the state of their illness at that time, and I thought it would be fitting to share it with our old friends. After returning home, I skimmed through it once and discovered that the ailment was some form of "persecution mania." The writing was jumbled and incoherent, filled with nonsensical statements. There were no dates mentioned, only variations in ink color and handwriting, indicating that it was not written all at once. However, there were some passages that provided some semblance of connection. I have now transcribed one of them for the purpose of medical research. I will not alter any errors in the text, as every word is precious. As for the names of individuals, although they are all villagers unknown to the world and are irrelevant to the overall context, I will change them all. As for the title of the book, it was given by the author after their recovery, and I will not change it. Recognized on April 2nd, seven years later.

CHAPTER 1

Tonight, the moonlight is beautiful.

I haven't seen him for over thirty years, but today, upon seeing him, I felt an extraordinary sense of relief. I only just realized that the previous thirty years were all filled with confusion. However, I must be extremely cautious. Otherwise, why would Zhao's dog look at me with disdain?

I have good reason to be afraid.

CHAPTER 2

Tonight, there is no moonlight, and I know it's not good. When I cautiously stepped out in the morning, Zhao Guiweng's gaze seemed strange. It appeared as though he feared me, as though he wished to harm me. There were also seven or eight people whispering and discussing me, afraid that I would notice. Everyone I encountered on the road was the same. Among them, the most malicious person smiled at me with an open mouth. I felt a chill run through my entire body, realizing that their plans had all been arranged.

But I am not afraid; I will continue on my way. A group of children ahead were also discussing me, their expressions mirroring Zhao Guiweng's, their faces turning pale. I wondered what grudge I held against those children for them to treat me this way. I couldn't help but shout loudly, "Tell me!" And they all ran away.

I think: What grudge do I have with Zhao Guiweng? What grudge do I have with the people on the road? Only twenty years ago, I kicked Mr. Gujiu's old ledger, and Mr. Gujiu was very unhappy. Although Zhao Guiweng didn't know him, he must have heard the rumors and stood up for justice. He made an appointment with the people on the road to be against me. But what about the children? At that time, they hadn't been born yet, so why do they look at me with strange eyes today, as if they're afraid of me, as if they want to harm me? This really scares me, surprises me, and makes me sad.

I understand now. It's what their parents taught them!

CHAPTER 3

I can never sleep at night. Everything needs to be studied in order to understand.

They — some of them have been punished by the magistrate, some have been slapped by the gentry, some have had their wives taken by the constables, some have had their parents killed by creditors; back then, their faces didn't have the same fear as yesterday, nor were they as fierce.

The strangest thing is the woman on the street yesterday who was beating her son. She said, "Father! I need to bite you a few times to vent my anger!" But she was looking at me. I was startled and couldn't hide it. The group of people with green faces and protruding teeth all burst into laughter. Chen Laowu came up and forcibly dragged me back home.

They dragged me home, and everyone in the house pretended not to know me. Their expressions were the same as everyone else's. When I entered the study, they closed the door and it felt like I was being locked up like a chicken or a duck. This whole situation makes it even harder for me to figure out the truth.

A few days ago, the tenant farmers from Wolf Village came to report the famine. They told my eldest brother that a notorious man in their village had been killed by everyone. They dug out his heart and liver, fried it in oil, and ate it to boost their courage. I made a comment, and both the tenant farmers and my eldest brother looked at me strangely. Today, I finally understand that their gaze is exactly the same as those outside.

Thinking about it, I feel chills from head to toe.

If they can eat people, then they might not hesitate to eat me.

Look at the woman's words, "bite you a few times," the laughter of the group of people with green faces and protruding teeth, and the words of the tenant farmers the day before yesterday. It's clearly a secret code. I see poison in their words and knives in their laughter. Their teeth are all sharp and white, the tools of cannibals.

In my own thoughts, although I'm not an evil person, things have become uncertain since I kicked Gu's ledger. They seem to have ulterior motives that I can't figure out. Moreover, as soon as they turn against someone, they label them as evil. I still remember when my eldest brother taught me about arguments, no matter how good a person is, if you criticize them a bit, he would draw a few circles around it. But if you forgive a bad person a few times, he would say, "Ingenious and unique." How could I possibly guess their true intentions? Especially when it's time for them to eat.

Everything needs to be studied in order to understand. It's been said that people have been eating each other since ancient times, I vaguely remember, but not very clearly. I opened a history book to check, but there were no dates in that history. Crooked and distorted, each page was filled with the words "benevolence, righteousness, and morality." I couldn't sleep straight and carefully read through the night until I could see the words through the gaps, and the entire book was filled with the words "eating people"!

So many words in the book, so many words spoken by the tenant farmers, all smiling and looking at me with strange eyes.

I am also a human being, and they want to eat me!

CHAPTER 4

In the morning, I sat quietly for a while. Chen Laowu brought in the meal, a bowl of vegetables, a bowl of steamed fish. The eyes of the fish were white and stiff, with their mouths open, just like those people who wanted to eat others. After eating a few bites, the slippery texture made it hard to tell if it was fish or human, so I vomited it out, along with its guts and intestines.

I said to Laowu, "Tell my eldest brother that I feel suffocated and want to take a walk in the garden." Laowu didn't respond and left. After a while, he came back and opened the door.

I didn't move either, studying how they would manipulate me. I knew they would never let their guard down. Sure enough, my eldest brother brought an old man slowly walking towards me. He had a fierce look in his eyes, trying to hide it by lowering his head and secretly glancing at me through the corners of his glasses. My eldest brother said, "You seem to be doing well today." I said, "Yes." My eldest brother said, "Today, Mr. He will come and examine you." I said, "Sure!" But I knew very well that this old man was disguised as an executioner! It was nothing more than an excuse to examine my pulse and assess my health: for this service, he would get a share of the flesh to eat. But I wasn't afraid; even though I don't eat people, my courage is stronger than theirs. I raised my fists, waiting to see what he would do. The old man sat down, closed his eyes, and felt for a long time, staying still for a while. Then he opened his ghostly eyes and said, "Don't think too much. Just rest quietly for a few days, and you'll be fine."

Don't overthink it, just rest quietly! If I fatten up, naturally they can eat more; what benefit do I have, how can it be "good"? These people, they want to eat others, but they are sneaky, trying to hide their intentions, afraid to make a direct move. It truly amuses me. I couldn't help but burst into laughter, feeling extremely happy. I know that within this laughter, there is righteousness and courage. The old man and my eldest brother both lost their composure, suppressed by my courage and righteousness.

But because I have courage, the more they want to eat me, the more they bask in a bit of that courage. As the old man stepped out of the door, not long after, he whispered to my eldest brother, "Quickly eat!" My eldest brother nodded. So it's you too! This revelation, although seemingly unexpected, was actually within my suspicions: the person conspiring to eat me is none other than my own brother!

My brother is the one who eats people!

I am the brother of a cannibal!

Even if I myself am being eaten, I am still the brother of a cannibal!

CHAPTER 5

These past few days, let's consider the possibility that the old man wasn't pretending to be an executioner, but a genuine doctor. He would still be a person who eats others. It is clearly written in their ancestral book, "Bencao something," by Li Shizhen, that human flesh can be fried and eaten. How can he claim he doesn't eat people?

As for my eldest brother, I won't accuse him unjustly. When he was teaching me, he explicitly mentioned the possibility of "changing children and eating them." Another time, when discussing a bad person by chance, he said not only should they be killed, but their flesh should be "consumed, and their skin used as bedding." At that time, I was still young, and my heart raced for a long time. When the tenant farmer from Langzi Village came to talk about eating hearts and livers the day before yesterday, my brother didn't find it strange at all, constantly nodding. It's clear that his mindset is just as cruel as before. Since "changing children and eating them" is possible, then anything can be changed, and anyone can be eaten. In the past, I used to listen to his reasoning and be confused, but now I understand that when he speaks of reason, not only does he have traces of human fat on his lips, but his heart is also filled with the intention to eat people.

CHAPTER 6

Pitch-black darkness, unable to distinguish day from night. Zhao's dog started barking again.

Fierce like a lion, timid like a rabbit, cunning like a fox...

CHAPTER 7

I understand their methods. They are unwilling to directly kill me, and they also dare not, fearing the consequences. So they all collaborate, spreading their nets, forcing me to commit suicide. Just observe the appearances of men and women on the streets these past few days, along with the actions of my eldest brother, and you can figure out eighty to ninety percent of it. It would be best to untie my belt, hang it from the beam, and strangle myself tightly. They would have no charge of murder, fulfilling their desires, naturally rejoicing with a sobbing laughter. Otherwise, scared to death with worries, even though I may be slightly thin, I can still nod in agreement a few times.

They are only capable of eating dead flesh! — I remember something written in a book, there is a creature called a "hyena," with an ugly appearance and gaze. It frequently consumes dead flesh, even grinding large bones into tiny pieces, swallowing them down. Just the thought of it is terrifying. "Hyenas" are relatives of wolves, and wolves are close relatives of dogs. The dog from Zhao's house gave me a few glances, indicating his collusion, already in contact. How could the old man hide it from me when he keeps looking down?

The most pitiful is my eldest brother. He is also a human, why is he not afraid? And why is he joining in eating me? Is it because he has always been accustomed to it, considering it normal? Or has he lost his conscience, intentionally committing such an act?

I curse those who eat people, starting with him. If I want to persuade those who have the inclination to eat people, I should start with him as well.

CHAPTER 8

In fact, by now, they should have already understood this reasoning...

Suddenly, a person arrived. He was around twenty years old, his appearance was not very clear, with a smile on his face. He nodded at me, but his smile didn't seem genuine. So I asked him, "Regarding the matter of eating people, is it true?" He continued to smile and said, "Unless it's a famine, why would people eat each other?" Immediately, I knew that he was also part of the group who enjoys eating people. This boosted my courage tenfold, and I insisted on questioning him.

"Is it true?"

"Why bother asking such a thing? You really know how to... tell jokes. The weather is nice today."

The weather is indeed good, and the moonlight is bright. But I want to ask you, "Is it true?"

He didn't think much of it. He hesitantly replied, "No..."

"Not true? How can they end up eating then?!"

"It's not true..."

"Not true? People in Langzi Village are eating right now, and it's written in books, vivid and recent!"

He immediately changed his expression, turning as cold as iron. With his eyes wide open, he said, "There have always been some, it has always been like this..."

"If it has always been like this, does that make it right?"

"I won't argue with you about these principles. In any case, you shouldn't say it. If you say it, then it's your fault!"

I jumped up, my eyes wide open, and the person was gone. I broke out in a large sweat. He was younger than my eldest brother, yet he was also part of the group; surely it was his parents who taught him. Perhaps they have already taught it to his son as well, that's why even the little children give me fierce looks.

CHAPTER 9

They themselves desire to eat people, yet fear being eaten by others, casting suspicious and deep glances at each other...

Once this mindset is gone, it feels so comfortable to do things, walk, eat, and sleep without worries. This is just a threshold, a crucial point. They are fathers, sons, brothers, husbands, wives, friends, teachers, students, enemies, and strangers, all forming a group, encouraging and restraining each other, unwilling to cross this line even in death.

CHAPTER 10

Early in the morning, I went to find my eldest brother. He stood outside the hall, gazing at the sky. I walked behind him, blocking the door, and spoke to him in an exceptionally calm and friendly manner.

"Elder brother, I have something to tell you."

"Just say it," he quickly turned his face and nodded.

"I only have a few words, but I can't say them. Elder brother, it seems that in the past, even savage people have eaten a bit of human flesh. But later, because of different thoughts, some stopped eating people and sought only goodness, truly becoming human. Some, however, continued to eat—like worms—and transformed into fish, birds, and monkeys, ultimately becoming human. Some never sought goodness and remain worms to this day. How shameful it is for those who eat people compared to those who don't! They are far, far more shameful than monkeys who are ashamed of being compared to worms.

"Yi Ya steamed his own son and fed him to Jie and Zhou, but that was an old story. Who would have known that from the time of Pangu's creation of the world, it continued to the son of Yi Ya, and from the son of Yi Ya, it extended to Xu Xilin, and from Xu

Xilin, it continued to the person caught in Langzi Village. Last year, in the city, they killed a criminal and even used a steamed bun dipped in blood to lick the disease-ridden person."

"They want to eat me, and as one person, you couldn't possibly think of a solution. But why should you join them? People who eat others are capable of anything. They will eat me, and they will eat you. Within the group, they will even devour each other. But as long as we take a step back, as long as we change immediately, then everyone can live in peace. Although it has always been like this, today we can choose to be especially good to each other. It's not impossible! Elder brother, I believe you can say it. The other day, the tenant farmers asked for a rent reduction, and you said it couldn't be done."

At first, he only sneered, but then his gaze turned fierce. As soon as I exposed their hidden secrets, his face turned pale. A group of people stood outside the gate, including Zhao Guiweng and his dog, peering in. Some had faces that couldn't be seen clearly, as if covered with cloth, while others still had their menacing appearance, smirking with closed lips. I knew they were all part of the group, people who eat others. But I also understood that their thoughts were different. Some believed that it had always been this way and that it was natural to eat others, while others knew it was wrong but still wanted to do it. They were afraid of being exposed, so upon hearing my words, they became even more furious, but they smirked with cold smiles.

At this moment, my elder brother also revealed a ferocious expression and shouted loudly, "Everyone, get out! What's there to see about a madman!"

At that moment, I understood their cunningness once again. Not only were they unwilling to change, but they had already made preparations to label me as the next madman. If they were to eat me in the future, not only would there be no trouble, but they might even gain sympathy. The story the tenant farmers told about everyone eating a wicked person was exactly this tactic. It was their old trick!

Chen Laowu walked in angrily. Despite efforts to silence me, I insisted on speaking to this group of people, "You can change, starting from genuine repentance! You should know that in the future, there will be no place for those who eat others to live in this world.

"If you don't change, you will devour each other as well. Even if you reproduce abundantly, you will eventually be eradicated by true humans, just like hunters exterminating wolves!—Just like worms!"

Chen Laowu drove away that group of people. I didn't know where my elder brother had gone. Chen Laowu advised me to go back inside the house. The interior was pitch-black. The beams and rafters trembled above me; after shaking for a while, they grew larger and piled up on top of me.

Extremely heavy, unable to move; his intention was for me to die. I knew his heaviness was fake, so I struggled and broke free, covered in sweat. But I insisted on saying, "You must change immediately, starting from genuine repentance! You should know that in the future, there will be no place for those who eat others..."

CHAPTER 11

The sun doesn't rise, the door doesn't open, and every day is just two meals. As I held the chopsticks, I thought of my elder brother; I knew that he was the reason for my sister's death. At that time, my sister was only five years old, with an adorable and pitiful appearance that still lingered in my mind. Mother couldn't stop crying, but he advised her not to cry; perhaps because he felt guilty for eating her. If he still had any guilt...

My sister was eaten by my elder brother, whether my mother knew or not, I couldn't say.

Mother probably knew, but she didn't explicitly mention it while crying, probably thinking it was inevitable. I remember when I was four or five years old, sitting in front of the hall to cool off, my elder brother said that if parents were sick, a son should cut off a piece of meat, cook it, and invite them to eat it in order to be a good person. Mother didn't object. If we ate a piece, then naturally we would eat the whole thing. But thinking back to that day's crying, it truly saddens me. It's an incredibly strange thing!

CHAPTER 12

I can't think about it anymore.

After thousands of years of cannibalism, today I finally understand that I have been mixed up in it for many years. My elder brother was in charge of the household affairs, and my sister coincidentally died. He might have secretly included her in our meals.

Perhaps, unintentionally, I didn't eat a few pieces of my sister's flesh, and now it's my turn...

With my four-thousand-year history of consuming human flesh, although I didn't know it at first, I now understand how rare it is to encounter a true human!

CHAPTER 13

Are there any children who haven't eaten human flesh?
Save the children...

April 1918.

KONG YIJI

The layout of the inn in Luzhen was different from elsewhere. It had a large counter in a curved shape facing the street, with hot water prepared inside for warming the wine. After the workers finished their work around noon or evening, they would often spend four copper coins to buy a bowl of wine. This was over twenty years ago; now the price has risen to ten coins per bowl. They would stand by the counter, drinking the warm wine to take a break. If they were willing to spend an extra coin, they could buy a plate of salted bamboo shoots or fennel beans as a snack to accompany the wine. If they spent more than ten coins, they could buy a meat dish, but most of the customers were from the lower class and couldn't afford such luxury. Only those who wore long robes would enter the adjacent room in the shopfront, ordering wine and dishes and leisurely sitting to drink.

Since I was twelve years old, I worked as a helper at the Xianheng Inn near the town's entrance. The boss said I looked too foolish and was afraid I couldn't serve the customers in long robes properly, so I should do some work outside. Although the customers outside, mostly in short jackets, were easier to deal with, there were also quite a few who were talkative and annoying. They often wanted to see with their own eyes as the yellow wine was ladled from the jar, check if there was water at the bottom of the pot, and personally witness the pot being placed in the hot water before they could feel at ease. Under such strict scrutiny, even pouring water became difficult. After a few days, the boss said I couldn't handle the job. Fortunately, due to the recommendation from someone important, I couldn't be dismissed and instead was assigned the monotonous task of warming the wine.

From then on, I would stand behind the counter all day, tending to my duty. Although there were no major mistakes, I always felt it was dull and boring. The boss had a stern face, and the customers never spoke kindly, making it impossible to be lively. Only when Kong Yiji came to the shop, could I hear a few laughs, and that's why I still remember him to this day.

   Kong Yiji was the only person who stood while drinking wine and wore a long robe. He was tall in stature, with a pale complexion and occasional scars between the wrinkles. His unkempt beard was a messy mix of white and gray. Although he wore a long robe, it was dirty and tattered, seemingly not repaired or washed in over a decade. When he spoke, it was always with a mouthful of incomprehensible words that left people half-understanding. Because his surname was Kong, others took a nickname for him from the half-understood phrase "Shangdaren Kong Yiji" on the red paper, and called him Kong Yiji. Whenever Kong Yiji entered the shop, all the drinkers would look at him and laugh. Some would call out, "Kong Yiji, you've got new scars on your face again!" He wouldn't reply but would say to the counter, "Two bowls of warm wine and a plate of fennel beans." Then he would pay with nine wen coins. They would deliberately shout loudly, "You must have stolen something from someone again!" Kong Yiji would widen his eyes and say, "How could you defame my innocence like this out of thin air..." "What innocence? I saw with my own eyes two days ago that you stole books from the He family and got caught." Kong Yiji's face would turn red, and veins would bulge on his forehead as he argued, "Taking books cannot be considered theft... Taking books!... Can it be called theft when it's a scholar's affair?" He would then continue with incomprehensible phrases like "gentlemen are often poor" and "this and that," which would make everyone burst into laughter. The atmosphere inside and outside the shop was filled with mirth.

   According to what people talked about behind his back, Kong Yiji had once studied books but never made it into school and didn't know how to make a living. As a result, he became poorer and poorer, to the point of begging for food. Fortunately, he had good calligraphy skills, so he would transcribe books for others in exchange for a bowl of rice to eat. Unfortunately, he had another bad habit: he enjoyed drinking and being lazy. After a few days, everything, including people, books, paper, and inkstone, would disappear all at once. After several incidents like this, there were no more people willing to have their books transcribed by him. Kong Yiji had no choice but to occasionally engage in petty theft. However, in our shop, his behavior was better than anyone else's, as he never owed any money. Although he sometimes didn't have cash on hand, we would temporarily note it on the chalkboard, but within a month, he would always repay the debt and his name would be wiped off the chalkboard.

After drinking half a bowl of wine, Kong Yiji's flushed face gradually returned to normal, and others asked him again, "Kong Yiji, do you really know how to read?" Kong Yiji looked at the person asking him with an expression of disdain and refused to argue. They continued, "How come you can't even pass the lowest-level scholar's exam?" Immediately, Kong Yiji appeared dejected and uneasy, his face turned gray, and he muttered some words. This time, they were all gibberish, incomprehensible phrases. At this moment, everyone burst into laughter, and the atmosphere inside and outside the shop was filled with mirth.

During these moments, I would join in the laughter, and the shopkeeper would never reprimand me. In fact, the shopkeeper would also ask Kong Yiji the same questions and find them amusing. Kong Yiji knew he couldn't engage in conversation with them, so he had no choice but to talk to children. Once he said to me, "Have you read books?" I nodded slightly. He said, "Since you've read books... let me test you. How do you write the character 'hui' in fennel beans?" I thought to myself, does a beggar like him have the right to test me? So, I turned my head away and ignored him. Kong Yiji waited for a while and said earnestly, "Can't write it?... Let me teach you, remember it! These characters should be remembered. When you become a shopkeeper, you'll need to use them for bookkeeping." I secretly thought that I was far from being a shopkeeper like him, and besides, our shopkeeper never recorded fennel beans in the accounts. I found it amusing and impatient, so I lazily replied, "Who needs you to teach? Isn't the character 'hui' just a horizontal stroke under a grass radical?" Kong Yiji looked extremely happy, tapping the countertop with the long nails of his two fingers and nodding, saying, "Right, right!... The character 'hui' has four different writing styles, did you know?" I became even more impatient, pouted, and walked away. Kong Yiji, who had just dipped his nails in the wine, wanted to write on the counter, but seeing my lack of interest, he sighed again, showing a great sense of regret.

Several times, neighboring children heard the laughter and joined in the fun, crowding around Kong Yiji. He would give them fennel beans, one for each child. After the children finished eating the beans, they still lingered, their eyes fixed on the plate. Kong Yiji became flustered, spreading his five fingers to cover the plate and bending down, saying, "There's not much left, I don't have much left." Standing up again and looking at the beans, he shook his head and said to himself, "Not much, not much! Is it too much? No, it's not much." Then, this group of children dispersed amidst laughter.

Kong Yiji was such a source of joy, but even without him, life went on as usual for everyone else.

One day, about two or three days before the Mid-Autumn Festival, the shopkeeper was slowly settling the accounts and removing the abacus from the counter. Suddenly, he said, "Kong Yiji hasn't come for a long time. He still owes nineteen coins!" It occurred to me that indeed he hadn't come for a long time. One of the drinkers said, "How could he come?... He broke his leg." The shopkeeper said, "Oh!" "He's still a thief. This time, he lost his mind and actually stole from the Ding family. Did he steal their things?" "What happened afterward?" "What happened? First, there was a trial, then there was a beating. They beat him throughout the night until he broke his leg." "And then?" "Afterward, his leg was broken." "What happened after his leg was broken?" "What happened?... Who knows? Maybe he died." The shopkeeper didn't ask any further questions and continued to slowly tally his accounts.

After the Mid-Autumn Festival, the autumn breeze grew cooler day by day, signaling the approach of early winter. I spent the whole day by the fire and had to put on a cotton coat. In the latter half of a day, there were no customers, and I found myself dozing off while sitting. Suddenly, I heard a voice, "Warm a bowl of wine." Though the voice was extremely low, it sounded familiar. I looked around, but there was no one in sight. When I stood up and looked outside, there was Kong Yiji sitting below the doorstep. His face was dark and thin, barely recognizable. He wore a tattered padded jacket, crossed his legs, and had a cushion underneath with a straw rope hanging from his shoulder. Upon seeing me, he said again, "Warm a bowl of wine." The shopkeeper also stuck his head out and said, "Kong Yiji? You still owe nineteen coins!" Kong Yiji looked dejected and replied, "I'll pay it off next time. This time it's cash, and I want good wine." The shopkeeper, as usual, joked, "Kong Yiji, did you steal something again?" But this time, he didn't argue much and simply said, "Stop making fun!" "Making fun? If you didn't steal, how did you break your leg?" Kong Yiji murmured, "I fell, fell, fell..." His eyes seemed to plead with the shopkeeper not to bring it up anymore. By this time, a few people had gathered, and both the shopkeeper and they laughed. I warmed up the wine and brought it out, placing it on the doorstep. Kong Yiji fumbled in his tattered pocket and took out four coins, which he placed in my hand. I noticed his hands were covered in mud, as he had used them to come here. Shortly after finishing his drink, he slowly walked away amidst the laughter and jokes of others.

Since then, I hadn't seen Kong Yiji for a long time. When the year-end approached, the shopkeeper took down the abacus and said, "Kong Yiji still owes nineteen coins!" The following year, on the Dragon Boat Festival, he said again, "Kong Yiji still owes nineteen coins!" But during the Mid-Autumn Festival, there was no mention of him, and neither did we see him during the year-end.

Until now, I haven't seen him — perhaps Kong Yiji has indeed passed away.

March 1919.

BLESSING

At the end of the lunar year, it truly feels like the end of the year. Not to mention in the villages and towns, even in the sky, the atmosphere of the upcoming new year is evident. Within the heavy gray evening clouds, flashes of light occasionally appear, followed by dull explosions, the sound of firecrackers being set off to send off the Kitchen God. The ones set off nearby are even more intense, with the deafening sound still lingering while the air is already filled with a faint smell of gunpowder. I am returning to my hometown, Lu Town, on this night. Although it's called my hometown, I no longer have a home, so I have to temporarily stay at the residence of Uncle Lu Si. He is a relative of mine, a generation older than me, and should be called "Fourth Uncle." He is an old scholar who studies the principles of Confucianism. He hasn't changed much, just a little older, but he still doesn't have a beard. When we met, we exchanged pleasantries, and after commenting that I had gotten "fatter," he immediately started cursing the New Party. However, I knew that he wasn't using it as an excuse to curse at me, because he was still criticizing Kang Youwei. Nevertheless, our conversation didn't really click, so before long, I found myself alone in the study.

The next day I woke up very late. After lunch, I went out to visit a few relatives and friends; the third day was the same. They hadn't changed much, just aged a bit. But everyone at home was busy, preparing for the "blessing." It was the grand ceremony at the end of the year in Lu Town, paying respects, welcoming the God of Fortune, and praying for good luck in the coming year. Chickens were slaughtered, geese were plucked, and pork was bought, meticulously cleaned. Women soaked their arms in water until they turned red, some even wore silver bracelets. After boiling, chopsticks were inserted haphazardly into these things, and they were called "blessing gifts." They were displayed until dawn, with incense and candles lit, respectfully inviting the gods of fortune to enjoy them. Only men were allowed to worship, and after worship, firecrackers were set off as usual. It was the same every year, in every household, as long as they could afford the blessing gifts and firecrackers, it would be the same this year. The sky became darker, and in the afternoon, it actually started snowing. The snowflakes were as big as plum blossoms, swirling in the sky, accompanied by mist and a bustling atmosphere, turning Lu Town into a mess. When I returned to Uncle Si's study, the roof tiles were already covered in white snow, making the room brighter. The large red "shou" character, a rubbing by Chen Tuan, was clearly displayed on the wall. One side of the couplet had fallen off and was loosely rolled up on the long table, while the other side remained, with the inscription, "Understanding principles brings harmony to the heart and mind." Feeling bored, I went to the desk under the window and saw a pile of incomplete Kangxi dictionaries, a collection of "Jinsilu" with annotations, and a book titled "Four Books with Annotations." In any case, I had made up my mind to leave tomorrow.

Besides, thinking about what happened when I encountered Xianglin's wife yesterday, I couldn't stay calm. It was in the afternoon when I visited a friend at the east end of the town. When I came out, I ran into her by the river. And from the gaze of her staring eyes, I knew she was clearly walking towards me. Among the people I met in Lu Town this time, no one had undergone such a drastic change as her: her graying hair from five years ago had turned completely white, making her look nothing like someone in their forties. Her face was gaunt, pale with a hint of black, and the previous expression of sadness had completely disappeared, as if she were a wooden sculpture. Only her eyes occasionally showed some vitality, indicating that she was still alive. She held a bamboo basket in one hand, empty except for a broken bowl. In the other hand, she leaned on a bamboo pole longer than herself, with a crack at the bottom. She had undoubtedly become a beggar.

I stood still, expecting her to ask for money.

"You're back?" she asked first.

"Yes."

"That's good. You can read and you've traveled around, seen a lot. I want to ask you something..." Her dull eyes suddenly lit up.

I never expected her to ask such a question, and stood there in surprise.

"It's... " She took a few steps closer, lowered her voice, and spoke in a secretive tone, "After a person dies, does their soul really exist?"

I was startled, and when I saw her eyes fixed on me, it felt like thorns were pricking my back. It was more anxious than facing an unexpected pop quiz in school, with the teacher standing right next to me. I had never really cared about the existence of souls, but how should I answer her now? In a brief moment of hesitation, I thought that people here generally believed in ghosts, yet she seemed doubtful—or rather, hopeful: hoping that they exist, yet hoping that they don't... Why should I add to the misery of someone facing the end? Perhaps it's better to say that they exist.

"Perhaps they do exist... I think," I stammered.

"So, there is also hell, then?"

"Ah! Hell?" I was very surprised and had to hedge my answer. "Hell? Logically speaking, there should be... But then again, maybe not... Who's to manage such things..."

"So, can the deceased family members meet each other?"

"Well, well, can they meet or not..." By now, I knew that I was still a complete fool. No matter how much I hesitated or planned, I couldn't resist three simple questions. I immediately became timid and tried to overturn my previous words, "That's... Actually, I can't say for sure... Whether souls exist or not, I can't say for sure."

I took advantage of her not asking further questions and quickly walked away, hastily escaping back to my uncle's house. I felt uneasy in my heart. I thought to myself that my answer might have been dangerous for her. Perhaps she felt lonely during other people's blessings, but could there be another meaning behind it? Or did she have some kind of premonition? If there were other implications and something happened as a result, then my answer would indeed bear some responsibility... But soon I laughed at myself, realizing that occasional incidents held no deep significance, and yet I was overthinking it. No wonder educators would say I had a nerve problem. Besides, I had already said "can't say for sure," overturning the entire premise of my answer. Even if something happened, it had nothing to do with me.

"Can't say for sure" is an extremely useful phrase. Courageous and impulsive young people often dare to provide answers to others' doubts, recommend doctors, but if the results aren't satisfactory, they usually become the scapegoat. However, by using "can't say for sure" as a conclusion, everything becomes carefree. At that moment, I felt the necessity of this phrase even more. Even when talking to a beggar woman, it was indispensable.

However, I still felt uneasy. Even after a night had passed, the memories kept resurfacing as if harboring some ominous premonition. In the gloomy snowy day, in the boring study, the uneasiness grew stronger. It's better to leave. I'll go to the city tomorrow. Is the clear stewed shark fin at Fuxing Building still one yuan per plate, both cheap and delicious? My former companions may have dispersed, but the shark fin is a must-try, even if it's just me... In any case, I had made up my mind to leave tomorrow.

Because I often saw things that didn't turn out as expected, I thought that this might not turn out as expected either. Sure enough, a special situation began. In the evening, I actually heard some people gathering in the inner room, seemingly discussing something. But soon, their voices stopped, and only my uncle continued to walk around and speak loudly:

"Not early, not late, but precisely at this time—this clearly shows it's an absurd situation!"

At first, I was astonished, then deeply unsettled, as if his words were related to me. I glanced outside the door, but no one was there. It wasn't until the workers came to make tea before dinner that I finally had a chance to inquire about the news.

"Just now, who was Four Uncle angry with?" I asked.

"Isn't it with Sister Xianglin?" the worker replied briefly.

"Sister Xianglin? What happened?" I quickly asked again.

"She's old."

"Did she pass away?" My heart suddenly tightened, almost

jumping, and my face probably changed color. But he never looked up, so he didn't notice. I calmed myself down and continued to ask:

"When did she pass away?"

"When? It was last night or maybe today. I can't say for sure," he replied.

"How did she die?"

"How did she die? She died from poverty," he casually answered, still not looking up, and then he left.

However, my panic was only temporary. As the anticipated event had already passed, I didn't need to rely on my own "can't say for sure" or his comforting explanation of "dying from poverty." I gradually felt at ease. But occasionally, there was still a hint of guilt. Dinner was served, and my uncle sat there solemnly. I still wanted to inquire about some news regarding Sister Xianglin, but I knew that even though he had read "The Goodness of Ghosts and Gods Lies in the Two Vital Energies," he had many taboos. It was absolutely forbidden to mention topics related to death or illness when approaching blessings. If there was no choice, one should use a substitute euphemism. Unfortunately, I didn't know what it was, so I kept wanting to ask but ultimately stopped myself. From his solemn expression, I suddenly suspected that he might think I was deliberately disturbing him at this particular time, and that was an absurd situation. So I immediately informed him that I would leave Lu Town and go to the city tomorrow to put his mind at ease. He didn't insist on me staying. We finished the meal in a dull atmosphere.

During the winter season, with its short days and snowy weather, the night had already enveloped the entire town. People hurried under the lamplight, but outside the window, it was quiet. Snowflakes fell onto the thick layer of snow, making a rustling sound that added to the sense of silence. I sat alone under the dim light of a vegetable oil lamp and thought about Sister Xianglin, this utterly boring woman who had been abandoned in the dust heap, seen enough as a worn-out plaything. Earlier, her form lay exposed in the dust heap, and from the perspective of those who lived interesting lives, they might have wondered why she still existed. Now, she had finally been cleaned away by impermanence. I didn't know if her soul existed or not, but in this world, the uninteresting didn't give birth, and even those tired of seeing her didn't see her anymore. For oneself and for others, it was all for the best. I listened quietly to the seemingly rustling sound of snowflakes outside the window and gradually felt a sense of relief.

However, the fragmented pieces of her life story that I had seen and heard so far finally came together.

She was not from Lu Town. In the early winter of one year, Four Uncle's family needed a new female worker, and it was Old Lady Wei, who worked in the middle, that brought her in. She wore a white headband, a black skirt, a blue padded jacket, and a pale gray vest. She was probably around twenty-six or twenty-seven years old, with a pale yellow complexion, but her cheeks were still rosy. Old Lady Wei called her Sister Xianglin and said she was a neighbor from her mother's side. Since the head of the household had died, she had come out to work. Four Uncle frowned, and Four Aunt already knew what he meant – she disliked that she was a widow. However, considering her appearance was decent and she seemed strong and obedient, not uttering a word out of turn, she was kept despite Four Uncle's frown. During the trial period, she worked all day, seeming bored when she had nothing to do, but she was strong and capable, almost surpassing a man. So, by the third day, it was decided that she would stay, earning a monthly wage of five hundred wen.

Everyone called her Sister Xianglin. No one asked her surname, but since Old Lady Wei said she was a neighbor, it was probably Wei. She wasn't much of a talker, only answering when others asked, and even then, her responses were brief. It was only after more than ten days had passed that it was gradually revealed that she had a strict mother-in-law at home, a younger nephew who was in his teens and could gather firewood, and that she had become a widow in the spring. He had also made a living by gathering firewood and was ten years younger than her. These were the only things that everyone knew about her.

The days quickly passed, but she never slackened in her work. Regardless of food or strength, she spared no effort. People said that Four Master Lu's house had employed a female worker who was even more diligent than hardworking men. By the end of the year, sweeping, mopping, slaughtering chickens, plucking geese, and staying up all night cooking festive dishes—she handled everything alone, without the need for additional laborers. Yet, she seemed content, with a smile gradually appearing at the corners of her mouth, and her face became fairer and plumper.

Shortly after the New Year, when she returned from washing rice by the riverside, she suddenly lost color and said that she had just seen a man wandering on the opposite bank, resembling her husband's uncle. She was afraid he had come to find her. Four Aunt was startled and tried to inquire about the details, but she remained silent. Once Four Uncle found out, he furrowed his brow and said, "This isn't good. She's probably escaped from something." And indeed, she had escaped, as this assumption was soon confirmed.

For about ten days afterward, everyone had gradually forgotten about the previous incident when Old Lady Wei suddenly brought in a woman in her thirties, saying she was Xianglin's mother-in-law. Although the woman had the appearance of a mountain dweller, she was quite composed in social situations and spoke with confidence. After exchanging pleasantries, she apologized and explained that she had come specifically to take her daughter-in-law back home because they were busy with spring affairs and there were only elderly and young members left in the household, and they needed more help.

"If her mother-in-law wants her to go back, then there's nothing more to say," Four Uncle said.

They settled the wages, totaling one thousand seven hundred and fifty wen, which she had all kept in the master's house and hadn't used a single penny. She handed everything over to her mother-in-law. The woman took the clothes, expressed her gratitude, and left. By then, it was already noon.

"Oh, the rice! Wasn't Sister Xianglin supposed to go wash the rice?" It took a while before Four Aunt exclaimed. She was probably feeling hungry and remembered it was lunchtime.

So everyone scattered to search for the rice basket. She checked the kitchen first, then the front hall, and finally the bedroom, but there was no trace of the rice basket. Four Uncle paced outside the door but couldn't find it either. It was only when he reached the riverside that he saw it placed neatly on the bank, with a vegetable plant next to it.

According to eyewitnesses, in the morning a white-covered boat had already docked in the river. The entire boat was covered, and no one knew who was inside, but no one paid attention to it beforehand. When Xianglin came out to wash the rice and was just about to kneel down, two men suddenly jumped out of the boat. They seemed like mountain folk, one of them grabbed her while the other assisted and dragged her into the boat. Xianglin cried out a few times, but afterward, there was no sound. They probably gagged her somehow. Then, two women approached, one was unrecognized, and the other was Old Lady Wei. Peeking into the cabin, it wasn't very clear, but it seemed like she was bound and lying on the boat's planks.

"Damn it! However..." Four Uncle said.

That day, Four Aunt cooked lunch herself, and their son, A'niu, tended the fire.

After lunch, Old Lady Wei came again.

"Damn it!" Four Uncle said.

"What do you mean? It's surprising that you dare to come see us again," Four Aunt said angrily while washing dishes. "You recommended her to us, and now you're collaborating to kidnap her. It caused such a commotion. What do people think when they see all this? Are you joking around with our family?"

"Oh my, oh my, I fell for it. This time, I came specifically to explain this. She came to me seeking a recommendation, and how could I have known that she was hiding it from her mother-in-law? I apologize, Four Master, Four Mistress. It's just that I sometimes get absent-minded and careless. I apologize for the inconvenience caused to the esteemed family. Luckily, your household has always been magnanimous and unwilling to quibble with petty people. This time, I will make sure to recommend a good replacement to make amends..."

"However..." Four Uncle said.

And so, the incident with Xianglin came to an end and was soon forgotten.

Only Four Aunt, because of the subsequent female workers they hired, most of whom were either lazy or gluttonous, or both, and not satisfactory in various ways, would occasionally bring up Xianglin. During these times, she would often mutter to herself, "I wonder how she's doing now?" It meant that she hoped Xianglin would come back. However, by the following year's New Year, she had given up hope.

As the New Year approached its end, Old Lady Wei came to pay her respects. She was already quite drunk and explained that she had gone back to her parents' home in Wei Family Mountain and stayed there for a few days, which is why she arrived late. Naturally, their conversation turned to Xianglin.

"Oh, her?" Old Lady Wei said with delight. "She's had good luck. When her mother-in-law came to take her back, it turned out she had already been promised to He Lao Liu from the He family, so not long after returning home, she was carried away in a bridal sedan chair."

"Oh my, what a mother-in-law!" Four Aunt exclaimed in astonishment.

"Oh my, my lady! You truly are the wife of a wealthy household. But for us mountain folk, from humble backgrounds, what does it matter? She has a younger brother-in-law who needs to get married too. If she doesn't marry him, where will they get the money for the betrothal gifts? Her mother-in-law is a shrewd and capable woman, quite scheming. So she married her off to the remote mountains. If she had married someone from our village, the dowry would not have been much. But there are few women willing to marry into the deep, wild mountains, so she received a bride price of 80,000. Now the second son's wife has also been married in, and the dowry cost only 50,000. After deducting the expenses for the wedding, there's still over 10,000 left. See, what a well-thought-out plan..."

"But did Xianglin agree?" Four Aunt asked.

"What does it matter if she agreed or not. - Everyone has to make a fuss, after all. As long as you tie them up with a rope, stuff them in the bridal sedan chair, carry them to the groom's house, put on the bridal crown, perform the wedding ceremony, and close the bedroom door, it's done. But Xianglin really went beyond the norm. I heard it was quite a fierce commotion, and people were saying it was probably because she had some connection with educated people in the past, which made her different. My lady, we've seen many cases: when a bride goes to her husband's home, there are those who cry and scream, those who threaten to kill themselves, those who make such a scene that they can't perform the proper rites, and even those who smash the wedding candles. But Xianglin was extraordinary. They say she howled and cursed the whole way, and by the time they reached the He family's estate, her throat was already hoarse. When they pulled her out of the sedan chair, the two men and her younger brother-in-law struggled to hold her down, but they still couldn't complete the wedding rites. In a moment of carelessness, they loosened their grip, and oh my, Amitabha, she banged her head against the corner of the incense table, leaving a big hole in her head. Blood gushed out, and even with two handfuls of incense ash and two pieces of red cloth, they couldn't stop the bleeding. It wasn't until they forcefully locked her and the men in the bridal chamber that she finally stopped cursing. Oh my, oh my, it was really..."

She shook her head, lowered her eyes, and fell silent.

"What happened afterward?" Four Aunt asked again.

"I heard she didn't get up the next day," she replied, raising her eyes.

"Afterward? — She got up. By the end of the year, she gave birth to a child, a boy who turned two during the New Year. During these few days I've been at my mother's house, someone went to the

He family's estate and came back saying they saw the mother and son there. Both were chubby, and there was no mother-in-law causing trouble. The husband was strong and capable, good at doing work, and they had their own house. Ah, she really had good luck."

From then on, Four Aunt no longer mentioned Xianglin.

But one autumn, about two New Year celebrations after the news of Xianglin's good fortune, she unexpectedly stood in front of Four Uncle's house again. On the table was a round basket filled with water chestnuts, and underneath the eaves was a small bundle. She still had the white headband tied around her head, a black skirt, a blue jacket, and a pale gray vest. Her complexion was pale and sallow, but the color had vanished from her cheeks. Tears streaked her eyes, and her gaze lacked the vigor it had before. And once again, it was Old Lady Wei leading her, appearing compassionate, as she chattered to Four Aunt:

"...This is truly an example of 'unexpected changes in life.' Her husband was a strong man, but who could have known that at such a young age, he would succumb to typhoid fever? He had already recovered, but after eating a bowl of cold rice, the illness relapsed. Fortunately, she had a son, and she was able to support herself by gathering firewood, picking tea leaves, and raising silkworms. She could have managed on her own, but who could have predicted that the child would be snatched away by a wolf? Spring is almost over, and now the wolves have come to the village. Who could have foreseen that? Now she's left with nothing but herself. The landlord came to collect rent and drove her away. She really has nowhere else to turn, so she had to come and seek help from the former master. Fortunately, she no longer has any other burdens, and it happens that the lady of the house is in need of someone, so I brought her here. I thought it would be better to have someone familiar rather than a complete stranger..."

"I was really foolish, truly," Xianglin's wife lifted her lifeless eyes and continued, "I only knew that when it snowed, the wild animals in the mountains wouldn't have food and would come to the village. I didn't know it could happen in spring too. Early in the morning, I opened the door and filled a small basket with beans. I asked our Ah Mao to sit on the doorstep and shell the beans. He was obedient, he listened to everything I said, and he went out. I was chopping firewood behind the house, rinsing rice, and when the rice was cooked, I was going to steam the beans. I called Ah Mao, but there was no response. I went out to look and saw beans scattered all over the ground, but no sign of our Ah Mao. He didn't go to play at someone else's house; we asked around, but he was nowhere to be found. I panicked and asked people to search for him. It wasn't until the afternoon that they found him in the mountains, lying in a grassy pit. His insides had been eaten empty, and he still tightly held that small basket in his hand..." She choked up, unable to form coherent sentences.

At first, Four Aunt hesitated, but after hearing her story, her eyes became slightly red. She thought for a moment and then instructed someone to bring a round basket and a mat to the lower room. Old Lady Wei seemed to have relieved a burden and let out a sigh of relief. Xianglin's wife appeared more at ease than when she first arrived. Without any guidance, she neatly arranged the mat herself. From then on, she worked as a female laborer in Lu Town.

Everyone still called her Xianglin's wife.

However, this time her situation changed significantly. Within two or three days of starting work, the employers noticed that she wasn't as agile as before, her memory was worse, and her face, like a dead body, remained devoid of any trace of a smile. Four Aunt's tone showed signs of dissatisfaction. When she first arrived, although Four Uncle furrowed his brow as usual, considering the difficulty of hiring female laborers, he didn't object much. He just quietly warned Four Aunt that although this person seemed pitiful, she was a bad influence on customs. It was fine to have her help, but when it came to ancestral worship, they didn't need her involvement. All the cooking had to be done by themselves, otherwise, it would be unclean, and the ancestors wouldn't eat it.

The most significant event in Four Uncle's household was the ancestral worship, and Xianglin's wife used to be busiest during those times. But now, she had leisure. The table was placed in the center of the hall, covered with a tablecloth, and she still remembered how to distribute the wine cups and chopsticks as before.

"Xianglin's wife, you leave it alone! I'll arrange it," Four Aunt said anxiously.

She awkwardly withdrew her hand and went to fetch the candlestick.

"Xianglin's wife, you leave it alone! I'll take care of it," Four Aunt said hurriedly.

She spun in a few circles, finally having nothing to do, and walked away in confusion. The only thing she could do on that day was to sit by the stove and tend to the fire.

The people in town still called her Xianglin's wife, but the tone and attitude were very different from before. They still spoke to her, but their smiles were cold. She paid no attention to those things, instead, she looked straight into their eyes and told her own story, which she never forgot day or night:

"I was really foolish, truly," she said. "I only knew that on snowy days, the wild beasts in the deep mountains wouldn't have food and would come to the village. I didn't know it could happen in spring too. Early in the morning, I opened the door and filled a small basket with beans. I asked our Ah Mao to sit on the doorstep and shell the beans. He was a very obedient child, he listened to every word I said, and he went out. I was chopping firewood behind the house, rinsing rice, and when the rice was cooked, I was going to steam the beans. I called, 'Ah Mao!' but there was no response. I went out to look and saw beans scattered all over the ground, but no sign of our Ah Mao. We asked around everywhere, but he was nowhere to be found. I panicked and asked people to search for him. It wasn't until the afternoon that a few people found him in the mountains, hanging on a thorny bush was one of his little shoes. Everyone said, 'It's over, he must have been attacked by a wolf.' We went further in, and sure enough, he was lying in a grassy pit, his insides had been eaten empty. Poor child, but he still tightly held that little basket in his hand..." She then shed tears, and her voice choked up.

This story had quite an effect. When men heard this part, they often suppressed their smiles and walked away uninterested. But women, instead of forgiving her, immediately changed their expression to one of disdain, and some even shed tears in solidarity. Some elderly women who hadn't heard her story in the street deliberately sought her out to listen to this tragic segment. They too shed tears when she reached the point of sobbing, sighed in sympathy, and left satisfied, while discussing it among themselves.

She simply repeated her tragic story to people over and over again, often attracting a small crowd of three or five to listen to her. But before long, everyone became familiar with it, and even the most compassionate old ladies who recited Buddhist scriptures no longer had a trace of tears in their eyes. Eventually, almost everyone in the town could recite her words, and hearing them became a headache-inducing annoyance.

"I was really foolish, truly," she would begin.

"Yes, you only knew that on snowy days, the wild beasts in the deep mountains would come to the village because they had no food," they would immediately interrupt her and walk away.

She stood there with her mouth agape, staring at them, and then she would also leave, seeming to realize that it was pointless. But she still deluded herself, hoping to bring up her Ah Mao's story by talking about other things like the little basket, beans, or other people's children. If she saw a two or three-year-old child, she would say:

"Oh, oh, if our Ah Mao were still here, he would be this big too..."

The children would be surprised by her gaze and tug on their mother's clothes, urging her to leave. So, she was left alone once again, and eventually, she would leave as well, having lost interest. Later, everyone knew about her temperament, and whenever a child was present, they would first ask her with a half-smile:

"Xianglin's wife, if your Ah Mao were still here, wouldn't he be this big too?"

She may not have known that her sorrow, after being chewed over and enjoyed by everyone for many days, had become worthless, deserving only annoyance and disdain. But from the shadow of people's laughter, she felt a sense of coldness and sharpness, and she no longer felt the need to speak. She would only glance at them without uttering a word.

Lu Town always celebrated the New Year, and it became busy after the 20th day of the twelfth lunar month. This time, Four Uncle's family needed to hire male laborers but still couldn't keep up with the work, so they asked Aunt Liu for help in slaughtering chickens and geese. However, Aunt Liu was a virtuous woman who followed a vegetarian diet and refused to take lives, so she only agreed to wash the utensils. Besides tending the fire, Xianglin's wife had nothing else to do and was left idle, sitting and watching Aunt Liu wash the utensils. Light snowflakes began to fall.

"Oh, oh, I was really foolish," Xianglin's wife looked at the sky, sighed, and murmured to herself.

"Xianglin's wife, you're at it again," Aunt Liu impatiently looked at her face and said, "Let me ask you: Isn't the scar on your forehead from when you bumped into something back then?"

"Uh, uh," she mumbled in response.

"Let me ask you: Why did you end up depending on it afterwards?"

"Me?..."

"Yes, you. I thought: you must have been willing to do it yourself, otherwise..."

"Ah, ah, you don't know how strong he is."

"I don't believe it. I don't believe that you, with your strength, could really resist him. You must have eventually agreed to it and now try to push the blame on his strength."

"Ah, ah, you... why don't you try it yourself?" She laughed.

Aunt Liu's wrinkled face also smiled, causing her to cringe like a walnut. Her dry little eyes glanced at Xianglin's wife's forehead and remained fixated on her gaze. Xianglin's wife seemed uncomfortable, immediately suppressing her smile, shifting her gaze, and looking at the snowflakes instead.

"Xianglin's wife, you really don't make sense," Aunt Liu said mysteriously. "It would have been better if you were a bit stronger, or even better if you had died from the impact. Now, you and your second man couldn't even live together for two years, but you ended up with a serious crime. Just think, when you go to the underworld in the future, those two dead men will still fight over you. Who will you give yourself to? The King of Hell will have to cut you into pieces and divide you among them. I think this is..."

A look of terror appeared on her face, something that had never been seen in the mountain village before.

"I think it would be better if you redeem yourself early. Go to the local temple and donate a doorstep as a substitute for yourself, let a thousand people step on it, ten thousand people cross it, to atone for your sins in this lifetime, so that you don't suffer after death."

At the time, she didn't say anything in response, but she was likely very distressed. The next morning, when she woke up, she had dark circles around her eyes. After breakfast, she went to the temple at the western end of the town to request permission to donate a doorstep. The temple priest initially refused, until she became so desperate that tears flowed, and he reluctantly agreed. The cost was twelve thousand copper coins.

She had long stopped talking to people because everyone was tired of Ah Mao's story. But ever since she talked with Aunt Liu, it seemed that the news had spread, and many people developed a new interest and came to tease her into speaking again. As for the topic, naturally, it changed to focus on the scar on her forehead.

"Xianglin's wife, let me ask you: How could you have eventually agreed to it back then?" someone said.

"Ah, what a pity, you hit it for nothing," another person looked at her scar and echoed.

She could tell from their smiles and tone of voice that they were mocking her, so she just stared at them without saying a word and eventually stopped looking back. She kept her lips tightly sealed, carrying the mark of shame on her forehead, and silently ran errands, swept the streets, washed vegetables, and hulled rice. Nearly a year passed before she finally withdrew her accumulated wages from Fourth Aunt, converting it into twelve silver dollars, and took leave to go to the western end of the town. However, before the next mealtime, she returned, looking content and her eyes shining brightly. She happily told Fourth Aunt that she had already donated the doorstep at the local temple.

During the Winter Solstice ancestor worship, she worked even harder, watching Fourth Aunt arrange the offerings and helping Ah Niu carry the table to the center of the hall. She confidently went to get the wine cups and chopsticks.

"You can leave it, Xianglin's wife!" Fourth Aunt hurriedly said in a loud voice.

She withdrew her hand as if it had been scalded, her face turning grayish-black. She no longer went to fetch the candlestick and just stood there absentmindedly. It wasn't until Fourth Uncle started the incense offering that he asked her to step aside, and she finally moved away. Her change this time was significant. The next day, not only did her eyes sink deeper, but her spirits also deteriorated further. She became very timid, not only afraid of the dark and shadows but even when she saw people, even her own family members, she always seemed nervous, like a mouse roaming around during daylight. Otherwise, she would sit still like a puppet. In less than half a year, her hair also turned white, and her memory became especially poor to the point where she often forgot to hull the rice.

"Why has Xianglin's wife become like this? It would have been better if we hadn't kept her," Fourth Aunt sometimes said this to her face, as if warning her.

However, she remained unchanged, showing no signs of improvement. They then thought of sending her away and told her to go back to Old Lady Wei's place. But when I was still in the town of Lu, it was only mentioned, and based on the current situation, it seems that it was finally put into practice. However, whether she became a beggar after leaving Fourth Uncle's house or if she went to Old Lady Wei's house first and then became a beggar, I do not know.

I was awakened by the loud firecrackers nearby and saw the bean-sized yellow lights. Then I heard the crackling of firecrackers, which was Fourth Uncle's family offering their blessings. I knew it was almost dawn. In a daze, I faintly heard the continuous sound of firecrackers in the distance, as if they were forming a dense cloud of sound throughout the day, accompanied by swirling snowflakes, embracing the entire town. In the midst of this bustling embrace, I felt lazy and comfortable. All the doubts from the day until early evening were swept away by the blessed air. I felt as if the heavens and earth and all the gods were enjoying the offerings of liquor and incense, stumbling drunkenly in the air, ready to bestow infinite happiness upon the people of Lu Town.

February 7, 1924.

TOMORROW

"No sound. What's wrong with the little one?" Red-nosed Lao Gong held a bowl of yellow wine and, as he spoke, gestured towards the adjacent wall. Blue-skinned Ah Wu put down his wine bowl and slapped his own back with all his might, mumbling vaguely, "You...you, you're thinking again..."

It turned out that Lu Town was a secluded place with some old-fashioned customs: before the first watch of the night, everyone would close their doors and go to sleep. There were only two households that stayed awake late into the night: one was Xianheng Inn, where a few friends gathered around the counter, enjoying food and drink; the other was the neighboring house of Widow Dan Si, who had been widowed two years ago and relied on her own hands to spin cotton yarn to support herself and her three-year-old son, so she slept late.

These past few days, there had indeed been no sound of spinning yarn. But since there were only two households awake in the late night, if there was any sound in Widow Dan Si's house, it would naturally be heard only by Lao Gong and the others. If there was no sound, it would also only be heard by Lao Gong and the others.

Lao Gong, having been slapped, felt quite comfortable and took a big gulp of wine, humming a little tune.

At this moment, Widow Dan Si was holding her precious child, sitting on the edge of the bed, with the spinning wheel quietly standing on the floor. The dim lamplight illuminated the child's face, which had a touch of blue amidst the crimson. Widow Dan Si calculated in her heart: she had already sought guidance from the divination sticks, made her wishes, and even tried herbal remedies. If there was still no improvement, what should she do? Perhaps she would have to consult Doctor He Xiao Xian. But the child's condition might be lighter during the day and worse at night. By tomorrow, when the sun rose, the fever would subside and the wheezing would ease. This was a common occurrence for sick people.

Widow Dan Si was a simple-minded woman who didn't understand the dreadfulness of the word "but." Many bad things, thanks to him, turned out well, but many good things also ended up ruined because of him. The summer nights were short, and not long after Lao Gong and the others finished their mournful singing, the eastern sky began to brighten. Before long, the slits in the window let in a silver-white dawn.

Widow Dan Si waited for daybreak, but it didn't come as easily for her. It felt incredibly slow, and each breath taken by her child seemed to last a year. Now, it was unexpectedly bright; the brightness of the sky overwhelmed the lamplight, and she could see her child's nostrils fluttering as they opened and closed.

Widow Dan Si knew it was not good. She secretly exclaimed, "Oh my!" and calculated in her mind: What should she do? There was only one option left, to consult Doctor He Xiao Xian. Though she was a simple-minded woman, she had determination in her heart. She stood up, took out the thirteen small silver coins and one hundred and eighty copper coins she had saved every day from the wooden cabinet, put them in her pocket, locked the door, and carried her child straight to the He family's house.

It was still early, but there were already four patients waiting at the He family's house. She took out a four-cornered silver coin, bought a numbered stick, and it was the fifth turn for her child. Doctor He Xiao Xian stretched out two fingers to feel the pulse. His fingernails were more than four inches long, which surprised Widow Dan Si inwardly. She calculated in her mind: Her child should have a chance at survival. However, she couldn't help but feel anxious and asked in a hurried manner, "Sir...what illness does my child have?"

"He has an obstruction in the middle burner."

"Is it serious? He..."

"First, let him take two doses of medicine."

"He can't catch his breath, and his nostrils are fluttering."

"This is a case of fire overacting on metal..."

Before Doctor He Xiao Xian finished his sentence, he closed his eyes. Widow Dan Si also felt embarrassed to ask further. Sitting across from Doctor He Xiao Xian was a man in his thirties who had already prepared a prescription. Pointing to a few characters on the corner of the paper, he said, "This first ingredient, the Infant-Preserving Life-Saving Pill, can only be found at the Jia family's renowned pharmacy!"

Widow Dan Si took the prescription and walked while thinking. Though she was a simple-minded woman, she understood that there was a connection between the He family, the renowned pharmacy, and her own family. Naturally, it would be more cost-effective to buy the medicine and return home. So she hurried to the renowned pharmacy. The shopkeeper, with his long fingernails, slowly examined the prescription and carefully packaged the medicine. Widow Dan Si held her child and waited anxiously. Suddenly, her child lifted a small hand and forcefully pulled at a strand of her disheveled hair. It was an action she had never seen before, and she was frightened.

The sun rose early. Widow Dan Si carried her child and the medicine bag, and the weight felt heavier as she walked. The child kept struggling, and the road seemed endless. Helpless, she sat on the doorstep of a mansion by the roadside to rest for a while. Her clothes gradually chilled her skin, and she realized that she was drenched in sweat. But her child seemed to be sleeping. When she got up and continued to walk slowly, still unable to support herself, she suddenly heard someone say by her ear, "Widow Dan Si, let me carry Bro Luo for you!" It sounded like the voice of Blue-Skin Ah Wu.

She looked up and saw that it was indeed Blue-Skin Ah Wu, who sleepily followed her. At this moment, although Widow Dan Si wished for a mighty warrior to lend a hand, she didn't want it to be Ah Wu. But Ah Wu had a bit of chivalry in him and insisted on helping no matter what, so after some refusal, she finally gave in. He extended his arms and reached directly from between Widow Dan Si's breasts and the child to pick up the child. Widow Dan Si suddenly felt a warmth spread on her breast, and in an instant, it spread to her face and ears.

The two of them walked together, leaving behind a distance of over two feet and five inches. Ah Wu talked, but Widow Dan Si mostly remained silent. After a short while, Ah Wu returned the child to her, saying it was time for him to meet his friends for a meal, as they had agreed upon yesterday. Widow Dan Si took back the child. Fortunately, they weren't far from home, and she had already seen Wang Jiuzheng's mother sitting by the street near their door. From a distance, she asked, "Widow Dan Si, what's wrong with the child? Have you seen the doctor?"

"I've seen him. Wang Jiuzheng's mother, you're older and have seen more. How about asking your experienced eyes to take a look and see how things are?"

"Hmm..."

"How is it...?"

"Hmm..." Wang Jiuzheng's mother examined the child for a while, nodded her head twice, and shook it twice.

By the afternoon, Bro Luo had taken the medicine. Widow Dan Si observed his expression, and it seemed somewhat stable. Suddenly, in the afternoon, he opened his eyes and called out, "Mom!" Then he closed his eyes again, as if falling back asleep. After a moment of sleep, sweat beads appeared on his forehead and nose, and when Widow Dan Si gently touched them, they stuck to her hand like glue. Anxiously, she touched his chest and couldn't help but sob.

Bro Luo's breathing went from stable to non-existent, and Widow Dan Si's voice changed from sobbing to wailing. At this point, several groups of people had gathered: inside the house were Wang Jiuzheng's mother, Blue-Skin Ah Wu, and others, while outside were the owner of Xianheng and Red-Nose Lao Gong, among others. Wang Jiuzheng's mother gave orders to burn a string of paper money and used two stools and five pieces of clothing as collateral to borrow two foreign dollars for Widow Dan Si to prepare meals for the helpers.

The first issue was the coffin. Widow Dan Si handed over a pair of silver earrings and a gold-wrapped silver hairpin to the owner of

Xianheng, asking him to keep them as collateral, and requested to buy a coffin partly in cash and partly on credit. Blue-Skin Ah Wu also reached out his hand, eager to volunteer, but Wang Jiuzheng's mother wouldn't allow it. She only allowed him to carry the coffin the next day. Ah Wu cursed, "Damn beast," and stood there sulking. The owner went on his way; he returned in the evening, saying that the coffin had to be custom-made and would be ready in the latter half of the night.

By the time the owner returned, the helpers had already finished their meal and left. Since there was still some old-fashioned tradition in Lu Town, people would go home to sleep before midnight. Only Ah Wu was still sitting by the counter of Xianheng, drinking, while Lao Gong hummed a tune.

At this moment, Widow Dan Si sat on the edge of the bed, crying, while Bro Luo lay on the bed and the spinning wheel stood silently on the ground. After a while, Widow Dan Si's tears came to an end. Her eyes widened as she looked around, feeling perplexed. She calculated in her mind, "It's just a dream. All of these things are just a dream. Tomorrow, I'll wake up and find myself sleeping peacefully on the bed, with Bro Luo sleeping soundly by my side. He'll wake up, call out 'Mom,' and play energetically."

Lao Gong's singing had long ceased, and Xianheng's lights were turned off. Widow Dan Si kept her eyes wide open, unable to believe everything that had happened. The rooster crowed, and the eastern sky gradually brightened as silver-white dawn seeped through the window cracks.

The silver-white dawn gradually turned crimson, and the sunlight illuminated the roof. Widow Dan Si sat there with wide-open eyes, in a daze. It was only when she heard a knocking sound on the door that she startled and ran to open it. Outside the door was an unfamiliar person carrying something on their back, with Wang Jiuzheng's mother standing behind them.

Oh, they had brought the coffin.

In the afternoon, it was only when Widow Dan Si cried and looked for a while, unwilling to accept it completely, that the coffin was finally closed. Fortunately, Wang Jiuzheng's mother became impatient and ran up angrily, dragging her away so that they could clumsily close it with seven hands and eight feet.

But Widow Dan Si had already done everything she could for her precious child, without any shortcomings. Yesterday, she burned a string of paper money, and in the morning, she burned forty-nine scrolls of the "Great Compassion Mantra." When preparing the body, she dressed him in new clothes and placed his favorite toys—a clay figure, two small wooden bowls, and two glass bottles—next to his pillow. Later, even Wang Jiuzheng's mother carefully pondered, pinching her fingers, but couldn't think of any deficiencies.

On this day, Blue-Skin Ah Wu was nowhere to be seen the whole day. So the owner of Xianheng hired two porters for Widow Dan Si, paying each two hundred coins plus ten extra large coins, to carry the coffin to the burial mound. Wang Jiuzheng's mother cooked a meal for them, and everyone who had lent a hand or spoken ate the meal. The sun gradually showed the colors of setting, and the people who had eaten also displayed the colors of going home, so they finally all went back home.

Widow Dan Si felt dizzy and rested for a while, and surprisingly, she felt a bit calmer. But then she started to feel something strange one after another: encountering things she had never encountered in her life, things that didn't seem possible but indeed happened. The more she thought about it, the more peculiar it became. And she felt another strange thing—the house suddenly became too quiet.

She stood up, lit a lamp, and the silence in the house became even more apparent. She walked dizzily to close the door, then came back to sit on the edge of the bed, and the spinning wheel stood quietly on the ground. She concentrated and looked around, feeling increasingly uncomfortable. Not only was the house too quiet, but it also seemed too big, and everything felt too empty. The excessively large house surrounded her from all sides, and the empty things pressed down on her, making it hard for her to breathe.

Now he knew for certain that his precious child was indeed dead. Unwilling to face the room, he blew out the lamp and lay down. He cried while thinking: remembering the times when he spun cotton yarn while his child sat by his side eating fennel beans, staring with his little black eyes and saying, "Mom! Dad sells wontons, and when I grow up, I will sell wontons too and make lots and lots of money—I'll give it all to you." At that time, even the cotton yarn he spun seemed to have meaning in every inch, as if it was alive. But what about now? Widow Dan Si really couldn't think of anything about the present situation. I've already mentioned before: she was a crude and foolish woman. What could she possibly think of? She just felt that the room was too quiet, too big, and too empty.

Although Widow Dan Si was crude and foolish, she knew that coming back to life was an impossible thing, and her precious child really couldn't be seen again. She sighed and muttered to herself, "My child, you should still be here. Come and visit me in my dreams." Then she closed her eyes, wanting to fall asleep quickly, to meet her precious child, and she listened attentively to his labored breathing, which passed through the stillness, the vastness, and the emptiness, clearly audible to her.

Widow Dan Si finally drifted off to sleep, and the whole house became very quiet. By this time, Red-Nosed Lao Gong's little tune had already finished singing. He staggered out of Xianheng, but his throat became hoarse again, and he sang:

"Oh, my enemy!—How pitiful you are,—all alone..."

Blue-Skin Ah Wu reached out and grabbed Lao Gong's shoulder, and the two of them laughed and stumbled away together.

Widow Dan Si had fallen asleep long ago, Lao Gong and his friends had left, and Xianheng had closed its doors. At this moment, the town of Lu was completely enveloped in silence. Only the dark night, longing to turn into tomorrow, still roamed within this stillness; and a few dogs hid in the darkness, whimpering and barking.

June 1920.

THE STORY OF HAIR

On a Sunday morning, I peeled off a calendar page from the previous day and looked at the new one, saying to myself as I examined it, "Ah, October 10th—today is actually Double Ten Day. But there's no mention of it here!"

A gentleman, Mr. N, who was my senior, happened to come to my dwelling for a casual chat. When he heard my remark, he became quite displeased and said to me, "They forget! They don't remember, so what does it matter if you remember or not?"

Mr. N had a somewhat irritable temperament and often got needlessly upset, saying things that lacked worldly wisdom. At times like these, I usually let him talk to himself and didn't respond. Once he finished his monologue, I considered the matter settled.

He continued, "I greatly admire the situation during Double Ten Day in Beijing. In the morning, the police would come to the doors and give the command, 'Raise the flag!' 'Yes, raise the flag!' Then, lazily, the majority of households would send out a citizen, unfurling a piece of faded and patchy foreign fabric. It would continue like this until nightfall—take down the flag and close the doors. Those who happened to forget would leave it hanging until the following morning."

"They forget to commemorate, and commemoration also forgets them!"

"I, too, am a person who forgets to commemorate. If I were to remember, the events before and after that first Double Ten Day would flood into my mind and make me feel restless."

So many faces of old friends would appear before my eyes. Several young men, after toiling for over ten years, had their lives taken by a hidden bullet. Some young men, missing their target with a single blow, suffered months of torture in prison. A few young men, filled with lofty aspirations, suddenly disappeared without a trace, their bodies unknown to this day.

They all lived their lives amidst society's cold sneers, insults, persecution, and entrapment. Now, their graves have gradually sunk into oblivion.

I cannot bear to remember these things.

"We can still talk about a little moment of pride."

N suddenly smiled, reached up to touch his own head, and said aloud, "What I'm most proud of is that since the first Double Ten Day, I haven't been laughed at or insulted while walking on the streets anymore.

"My friend, do you know that hair is both a treasure and a trouble for us Chinese people? Throughout history, how many of us have suffered pointless hardships because of it!

"Our ancient ancestors seemed to have regarded hair lightly as well. According to the laws at the time, the most important thing was the head, which is why decapitation was the ultimate punishment. The next important thing was the genitals, which is why castration and confinement were terrifying penalties. As for shaving the head, it was relatively insignificant. However, when you think about it, you realize that countless individuals have had their lives trampled upon by society simply because they were bald.

"When we talk about revolution, we often mention the Ten Days of Yangzhou and the Massacre of Jiaxing, but in reality, they were just means to an end. Honestly speaking, the resistance of the Chinese people at that time wasn't due to the loss of their nation but because of their refusal to cut their queues.

"After the stubborn rebels were eliminated and the old people died of old age, the queues remained, and then the Boxers rose up again. My grandmother once told me that during that time, it was difficult to be an ordinary citizen. Those who kept their hair were killed by the imperial soldiers, and those with queues were slaughtered by the rebels!

"I don't know how many Chinese people have suffered, endured hardships, and perished just because of this insignificant hair."

N gazed at the ceiling, seemingly lost in thought, and continued, "Who would have thought that I would experience the hardships of hair as well?

"When I went abroad to study, I cut off my queue. There was nothing profound about it; it was just inconvenient. However, some of my classmates who still had their queues coiled on top of their heads detested me for it. The supervisor became furious and threatened to cut off my funding and send me back to China.

"Not long after, that very same supervisor had his own queue cut off, and he fled. Among the people who cut off his queue was Zou Rong, who wrote The Revolutionary Army. Because of this incident, he was no longer able to study abroad and returned to Shanghai, where he later died in prison. Have you also forgotten about it?"

"After a few years, my family's situation worsened, and if I didn't come up with something to do, I would go hungry. So, I had to return to China as well. As soon as I arrived in Shanghai, I bought a fake queue, which was priced at two yuan at the time, and brought it home. My mother didn't say much about it, but whenever others saw me, they would immediately scrutinize the queue. Once they realized it was fake, they would let out a cold laugh and accuse me of deserving execution. One relative even contemplated reporting me to the authorities but eventually stopped, fearing the success of the revolutionary party's rebellion.

"I thought to myself, 'Fake is never as good as the real thing,' so I decided to abandon the fake queue and walk the streets wearing a Western suit. As I walked, I was met with laughter and insults the entire way. Some even followed behind me, cursing, 'What an audacious fellow!' 'Fake foreign devil!'

"So, I stopped wearing Western clothes and switched to a gown, but they insulted me even more vehemently. When I was at my wit's end, I finally obtained a walking stick, and I fiercely struck it a few times. Gradually, they stopped insulting me. However, whenever I walked into an area where I hadn't struck anyone, they resumed their insults.

"This incident filled me with sorrow, and I still remember it vividly to this day. During my time studying abroad, I once read in the newspaper about Dr. Honda's journey to Nanyang and China. Dr. Honda didn't understand Chinese or Malay, so when people asked him how he managed to get around, he held up his walking stick and said that it was their language, and they all understood it! This made me furious for several days, but little did I know that I would unknowingly do the same thing, and those people would understand it as well...

"In the early years of the Xuantong period, I worked as a supervisor in a local middle school. My colleagues kept their distance from me out of fear, and the bureaucrats were overly cautious with me. I felt as though I were sitting in an ice cellar or standing beside an execution ground all day, all because I lacked a queue!

"One day, a few students suddenly entered my room and said, 'Teacher, we want to cut off our queues.' I said, 'No!' 'Is it better to have a queue or not?' 'It's better not to have a queue...' 'Then why do you say no?' 'It's unnecessary. It's better if you don't cut it off... Wait a bit.' They didn't say anything and walked out with pouted lips. However, they eventually cut them off.

"Oh, it caused quite a stir. People were whispering, but I pretended not to know and continued teaching in the classroom with my bald head alongside many queues."

"However, this epidemic of cutting off queues spread. On the third day, students from the Normal School suddenly cut off six queues, and they were expelled that evening. These six individuals couldn't stay at school or go home. They endured until after the first Double Tenth Festival, over a month later, for the branding of their crimes to fade away.

"What about me? It was the same for me. But when I went to Beijing in the winter of the first year, I was insulted a few times. Later, the people who insulted me had their queues cut off by the police, and I was no longer subjected to humiliation. However, I didn't go to the countryside."

N appeared extremely proud, but then his face grew solemn.

"And now you idealists, what are you clamoring about women cutting their hair? You want to create many miserable individuals who gain nothing from it!

"Now, aren't there already women who have cut their hair and can't get admitted to school or have been expelled from school?

"Reform, you say? Where are the weapons? Vocational education, you say? Where are the factories?

"Still, they want them to stay and get married as daughters-in-law. Forgetting everything is happiness. But if she remembers a few words about equality and freedom, she will suffer for a lifetime!

"I want to borrow the words of Al-Jahiz-Basuyev to ask you: You promise the coming of a golden age to the descendants of these people, but what do you give to these people themselves?

"Ah, as long as the whip of creation hasn't struck the spine of China, China will forever remain the same, refusing to change even a single strand of hair!

"Since your mouths have no venomous fangs, why do you insist on sticking the words 'viper' on your foreheads, enticing beggars to come and kill you?..."

N's words became increasingly bizarre, but as soon as he noticed my reluctant expression, he immediately fell silent, stood up, and took his hat.

I asked, "Are you leaving?"

He replied, "Yes, it's going to rain."

I silently accompanied him to the door.

He put on his hat and said, "Goodbye! Please forgive me for disturbing you. Fortunately, tomorrow is not the Double Tenth Festival, and we can forget about it."

October 1920.

AT THE RESTAURANT

I was traveling southeast from the northern region and took a detour to visit my hometown, which led me to the city of S. This city was only thirty miles away from my hometown, and it took half a day by boat to reach it. I had taught at a school here for a year. In the deep winter after the snow, the scenery was desolate, and a feeling of laziness and nostalgia intertwined within me. I ended up staying temporarily at the Lousi Hotel in S city, which was newly established. The city was not big, and I visited several old colleagues whom I thought I could meet, but none of them were around. They had dispersed, and I didn't know where they had gone. Passing by the entrance of the school, it had changed its name and appearance, unfamiliar to me. In less than two hours, my enthusiasm had already waned, and I regretted coming here for such trivial matters.

The hotel I stayed in only rented rooms and didn't provide meals, so I had to order food separately. However, the food was tasteless, like chewing on mud. Outside the window, there were only stained and weathered walls covered with dead moss. Above was a leaden-colored sky, bleak and devoid of any excitement, and light snowflakes were falling again. I hadn't had a satisfying lunch, and there was nothing to occupy my time, so I naturally thought of a familiar little restaurant I had known before called Yishiju, which wasn't far from the hotel. I immediately locked my room door and headed towards that restaurant. Actually, my intention was merely to temporarily escape the boredom of being a guest, not specifically to get drunk.

Yishiju was still there, with its narrow and damp storefront and worn-out signboard. However, from the owner to the waiters, there was not a single familiar face. I had become a complete stranger in this Yishiju. Nevertheless, I finally ascended the familiar staircase in the corner and reached the upper floor, where there were still five small wooden tables. Only the back window, which used to have wooden frames, had been replaced with glass.

"One jin of Shao wine. Any dishes? Ten fried tofu, with extra spicy sauce!"

While speaking to the waiter who had come up with me, I walked towards the back window and sat down at a table next to it. Upstairs was "empty and vacant," allowing me to choose the best seat that offered a view of the deserted garden below. This garden probably did not belong to the restaurant; I had often gazed at it before, even on snowy days. However, now, looking at it with my accustomed northern eyes, I found it astonishing. Several old plum trees were blooming with abundant flowers, defying the deep winter as if they were completely indifferent to it. Next to the collapsed pavilion, there was even a camellia tree, displaying over a dozen red flowers amidst its dark green foliage. They shone brightly in the snow, fierce, proud, and seemingly scornful of the willingly ignorant travelers embarking on distant journeys. At that moment, I suddenly thought about the nourishment of the accumulated snow here. It didn't melt away, glistening with a luminous quality, unlike the dry powder of the snow in the north. With a strong gust of wind, it would fly through the air like smoke.

"Customer, here's your wine..."

The lazy waiter said as he placed down the cup, chopsticks, wine jug, and dishes. The wine arrived. I turned my face towards the wooden table, arranged the utensils, and poured the wine. I felt that although the north was not my hometown, coming from the south only made me a guest. Regardless of how the dry snow might be falling there or how the soft snow here showed its attachment, it didn't matter to me anymore. I felt a hint of melancholy but also a sense of comfort as I took a sip of the wine. The taste of the wine was pure, and the fried tofu was cooked perfectly. It was a pity that the spicy sauce was too weak; the people of S city were not accustomed to eating spicy food.

Perhaps it was because it was still afternoon, this restaurant, despite being called a "wine house," lacked the atmosphere of one. I had already consumed three cups of wine, and the other four tables remained empty. As I looked at the deserted garden, I gradually felt a sense of loneliness, but I also didn't want any other customers to join me. When I heard footsteps on the stairs by chance, I couldn't help but feel annoyed. However, when I saw that it was the waiter, I felt relieved, and I had another two cups of wine in this manner.

I thought to myself, "This time it must be another customer," as I could hear the footsteps much slower than those of the waiter. As soon as I estimated that he had reached the top of the stairs, I anxiously looked up to see this unexpected companion. At the same time, I was surprised and stood up. I never expected to encounter a friend here, assuming he still considered me a friend. The person who came up was undoubtedly my old classmate and former colleague during our teaching days. Although his appearance had changed somewhat, I recognized him immediately. Only his movements had become unusually slow, unlike the agile and vigorous Lü Weifu of the past.

"Ah, Weifu, is it really you? I never expected to meet you here."

"Ah, is it you? I also never expected..."

I invited him to sit with me, but he seemed slightly hesitant before finally taking a seat. I found it strange at first, then somewhat saddened and displeased. Looking closely at his face, his hair was still untidy, and his pale rectangular face had become thinner. He appeared calm, or perhaps rather dejected. The eyes beneath his thick and dark eyebrows had lost their sparkle, but as he slowly glanced around, a gleam reminiscent of the piercing gaze I often saw during our school days suddenly emerged when he looked at the deserted garden.

"We..." I said with joy, yet somewhat awkwardly, "It must have been around ten years since we last parted ways. I knew you were in Jinan, but I was too lazy to make the effort and ended up not writing a letter..."

"The same goes for both of us. But now I'm in Taiyuan, it has been over two years, with my mother. When I came back to pick her up, I learned that you had already moved away, leaving everything behind."

"What are you doing in Taiyuan?" I asked.

"Teaching, at a fellow villager's house."

"And before that?"

"Before that?" He took out a cigarette from his pocket, lit it, placed it between his lips, and watched the smoke rise. In a contemplative tone, he said, "I did some boring things, equivalent to doing nothing at all."

He also asked about my situation after our separation. While giving him a general overview, I asked the waiter to bring cups and chopsticks, allowing him to have some of my wine first before adding two more jin. In the meantime, we ordered dishes. Previously, we had been straightforward and unceremonious, but at this moment, we both declined, unable to determine who initiated the order. Eventually, we settled on four dishes based on the waiter's verbal recommendation: fennel beans, cured meat, fried tofu, and dried fish.

"When I returned, I realized how ridiculous I was," he said, holding the cigarette in one hand and supporting the wine glass with the other, smiling or rather half-smiling at me. "When I was young, if I saw a bee or a fly land somewhere and got scared by something, it would immediately fly away. But after flying a small circle, it would come back and land in the same spot. I thought it was really funny and also pitiful. But unexpectedly, now I've flown back as well, just with a slight detour. And unexpectedly, you've also come back. Can't you fly even farther?"

"That's hard to say, maybe we're just flying in a few small circles," I replied, also with a half-smile. "But why did you fly back?"

"Still for boring things," he said, emptying a glass of wine in one gulp, taking a few puffs of smoke, his eyes widening slightly. "Boring things. But let's talk about it."

The waiter brought the newly added wine and dishes, filling the table. The smoke from the cigarettes and the warmth of the fried tofu filled the room, as if it had become lively. Outside, the snow continued to fall more heavily.

"Perhaps you already knew," he continued, "I had a younger brother who died at the age of three and was buried in this countryside. I can't even remember what he looked like, but according to my mother, he was a very cute and likable child. Even now, she almost sheds tears when she mentions him. This spring, a cousin sent a letter saying that his grave was gradually being submerged in water and was in danger of sinking into the river. We needed to hurry and do something about it. My mother was very worried as soon as she found out, she could hardly sleep for several nights. She read the letter herself. But what could I do? I had no money, no time: at that time, I had no means at all."

"Until now, taking advantage of the holiday break, I finally came back to the south to relocate his grave," he said, emptying another glass of wine, looking out the window and saying, "How can it be like that over there? Flowers grow in the snow, and the ground beneath the snow doesn't freeze. Just the day before yesterday, I bought a small coffin in the city because I anticipated that what was buried there must have decayed long ago. I brought cotton and blankets, hired four laborers, and went to the countryside to relocate the grave. At that moment, I suddenly felt very happy, willing to dig a grave, willing to see the remains of my younger brother who had been close to me. These were experiences I had never had in my life. When we arrived at the gravesite, indeed, the river water had only bitten into it, just two feet away from the grave. The pitiful grave had not been covered with soil for two years and had leveled down. I stood in the snow and decisively pointed at it, saying to the laborers, 'Dig it open!' I truly am an ordinary person, and at that moment, I felt that my voice sounded strange, and that command was one of the greatest commands in my life. But the laborers weren't surprised at all and started digging. When the grave was dug, I went over to look, and sure enough, the coffin was almost completely rotten, leaving only a pile of wood fibers and small wood fragments. My heart trembled, and I carefully removed them, wanting to see my younger brother. However, to my surprise! There was nothing — no bedding, no clothes, no bones. I thought maybe they had all disappeared. I had heard that hair is the hardest to decay, so perhaps it was still there. I bent down and carefully examined the soil where the pillow should have been, but there was nothing. Not a trace!"

Suddenly, I noticed his eyes were slightly red, but I immediately knew it was due to the alcohol. He didn't eat much, just kept drinking wine. He had already consumed over a catty (a Chinese unit of weight), and his expression and movements became lively, resembling the Lu Weifu I had known before. I asked the waiter to add another two catties of wine, then turned around, holding my wine glass, and silently faced him, listening.

"To be honest, there was no need to relocate it anymore. We could have simply leveled the ground, sold the coffin, and called it a day. Selling the coffin might seem peculiar, but as long as the price was extremely cheap, the original shop would have taken it, and I could have at least recovered a few coins for wine money. But I didn't do that. I still laid down the bedding, wrapped some soil from the place where his body had been before with cotton, wrapped it up, put it in a new coffin, and transported it to the grave where my father was buried, burying it next to him. Because the outside was bricked up, I was busy as a foreman yesterday for most of the day. But in this way, I finally finished something, enough to deceive my mother and put her mind at ease. Ah, why do you look at me like that? Do you wonder why I am so different from before? Yes, I still remember when we went to the City God Temple to pluck the beard of the deity and discussed day after day the methods to reform China, even getting into fights. But now, this is how I am — half-hearted, vague, and confused. Sometimes I think to myself, if my old friends were to see me, they might not recognize me as their friend anymore. However, this is how I am now."

He took out another cigarette, placed it between his lips, and lit it.

"Judging by your expression, it seems you still have some expectations of me. I've naturally become more numb now, but some things can still be discerned. It makes me grateful, but it also makes me uneasy, afraid that I have ultimately let down old friends who still harbor good intentions towards me..." He suddenly paused, took a few puffs of his cigarette, and then slowly continued, "Just today, right before I came to this stone house, I did something trivial, but it was something I willingly did. My former neighbor to the east, Changfu, is a boatman. He has a daughter named Ashun, whom you may have seen when you came to my house, but you probably didn't pay attention because she was still young at that time. Later on, she didn't grow up to be particularly attractive, just an ordinary, slender face with a yellow complexion. The only notable feature was her very large eyes, with long eyelashes and bright blue irises like a clear night sky in the north, which is not as bright and clear here. She was very capable. By her early teens, she had lost her mother and took care of her two younger siblings. She also had to serve her father and was meticulous in everything. She was also economical, and the family's finances gradually became stable. Almost every neighbor praised her, and even Changfu often expressed his gratitude. This time when I left to come back, my mother remembered her again. The memory of elderly people is truly long-lasting. My mother said she once knew that Shungu saw someone wearing a red velvet flower on their head and wanted one for herself. When she couldn't get it, she cried, crying for almost half the night, and then received a beating from her father. Her eye sockets were swollen and red for two or three days afterward. Those velvet flowers are things from another province. Even in the city of S, they couldn't be bought. How could she get them? So, taking advantage of my trip back to the south this time, she asked me to buy two flowers and give them to her."

"I wasn't annoyed by this errand at all; in fact, I quite liked it. For Ashun, I still had some willingness to make an effort. Two years ago, when I came back to pick up my mother, one day I happened to have a casual conversation with Changfu at his home. He insisted on treating me to some snacks, buckwheat flour, and he even told me that he added white sugar. You see, a boatman who has white sugar at home must not be a poor boatman, so he ate quite extravagantly. I couldn't refuse his offer, but I requested a small bowl. He was quite worldly-wise and instructed Ashun, 'They literary folks don't eat much. Give him a small bowl, but add plenty of sugar!' However, when the bowl was brought to me, it still startled me. It was a large bowl, enough to last me a whole day. But compared to the bowl Changfu ate from, mine was indeed a small bowl. I had never eaten buckwheat flour before, and this time, it was truly unappetizing, but extremely sweet. I mindlessly took a few bites and thought of not eating anymore. However, unintentionally, I suddenly saw Ashun standing in the corner of the room, and it immediately made me lose the courage to put down my chopsticks. I observed her expression, which seemed fearful yet hopeful, probably afraid that she hadn't seasoned it well and hoping that we would enjoy the taste. I knew that if I left more than half the bowl, it would surely disappoint her and make her feel sorry. So I made up my mind, opened my throat, and gulped it down, almost as quickly as Changfu ate. It was then that I realized the suffering of forcing oneself to eat. I only remembered experiencing such difficulty when I was a child, eating a whole bowl of sand sugar mixed with deworming powder. However, I didn't complain because the satisfied smile she restrained while collecting the empty bowl was more than enough compensation for my discomfort. So, even though I felt bloated and couldn't sleep well that night and had a string of nightmares, I still wished her a lifetime of happiness and hoped the world would become better for her. However, these thoughts were merely remnants of my old dreams, and I immediately laughed at myself and subsequently forgot about them.

"I didn't know before that she had been beaten for a velvet flower, but when my mother mentioned it, I also remembered the incident with the buckwheat flour. Unexpectedly, I became diligent. I searched throughout the city of Taiyuan, but found nothing. It was only until Jinan..."

Outside the window, there was a rustling sound as a lot of accumulated snow slid down from a branch of the camellia tree he had bent. The branches straightened up, highlighting the glossy, dark green leaves and the blood-red flowers. The leaden gray of the sky became even denser. Birds chirped and tweeted, indicating that dusk was approaching. The ground was once again covered in snow, and unable to find any food, they all returned to their nests to rest.

"It was only until Jinan," he looked out the window for a moment, turned around, drank a glass of wine, took a few puffs of his cigarette, and continued, "that I finally managed to buy a velvet flower. I don't know if it was the same kind that made her get beaten, but it was made of velvet, at least. I didn't know if she preferred dark or light colors, so I bought one in bright red and another in pink, and I brought them here.

"Just this afternoon, right after I finished eating, I went to see Changfu. I purposely delayed it for a day. His house was still there, though it looked somewhat gloomy, but that might just be my own perception. His son and the second daughter, Azhao, were standing at the door. They had grown up. Azhao didn't resemble her sister at all; she looked more like a ghost. But when she saw me approaching their house, she sprinted inside. I asked the boy where Changfu was. He immediately widened his eyes and repeatedly asked me why I was looking for his older sister, and he seemed to be viciously about to pounce on me and bite me. I stammered and retreated. Now, I'm just doing things half-heartedly...

"You don't know, but I'm even more afraid of visiting people than before. Because I have come to despise myself, even despise myself, so why deliberately make someone secretly unhappy when I know it? However, this errand cannot be left unfinished, so after thinking it over, I finally went back to the firewood shop just across the street. The owner's mother, Grandma Lao Fa, was still there, and she recognized me. She even invited me to sit inside the shop. After exchanging a few pleasantries, I explained the reason for my return to S City and my search for Changfu. Unexpectedly, she sighed and said, 'Unfortunately, Shun Gu doesn't have the fortune to wear this velvet flower.'"

"She then told me in detail. She said that 'since last spring, she had been getting thin and yellow. Later, she started crying frequently, but when asked about the reason, she wouldn't say. Sometimes, she would cry all night, crying so much that even

Changfu couldn't help getting angry and scolding her, saying she had gone crazy due to her old age. But when autumn came, it started with just a minor cold, and eventually, she fell ill and couldn't get up. It wasn't until a few days before she passed away that she finally confessed to Changfu that she had been spitting blood and having night sweats, just like her mother. But she kept it a secret, afraid that he would worry. One night, her uncle Changgeng came to forcefully borrow money — this was a common occurrence — and she refused. Changgeng sneered and said, 'Don't be so arrogant. Your man is even worse than me!' From that moment on, she became distressed and embarrassed, unable to ask directly and could only cry. Changfu hurriedly told her about the insulting things her man had said, but what was the point? Besides, she didn't believe it and even said, 'It's fortunate that I'm already like this, nothing matters anymore.'"

"She also said, 'If her man is truly worse than Changgeng, then that's truly terrifying! What is he compared to a chicken thief? However, when he came to pay his respects, I saw him with my own eyes. His clothes were clean, and he looked respectable. He even had tears in his eyes, saying he had worked hard his whole life, saving up money to hire a woman, only for her to die. It's evident that he is a good person, and everything Changgeng said was a lie. It's just a pity that Shun Gu actually believed such a deceitful scoundrel's words and lost her life for it. But we can't blame anyone for that, we can only blame Shun Gu herself for not having that good fortune.'"

"That's all for my business. But what should I do with the two velvet flowers I have with me? Alright, I'll have her give them to Azhao. Whenever Azhao sees me, she runs away as if she's seeing a wolf or something. I really don't want to give them to her. But I'll still give them, just telling her mother that Azhun really likes them. These trivial matters mean nothing. Just muddle through. Muddle through the New Year and continue teaching me 'The Analects say, "Poems cloud..."'

"Are you teaching something like 'Confucius said, The Book of

Songs says'?" I felt curious, so I asked.

"Of course. Did you think I was teaching ABCD? At first, I had two students, one reading 'The Book of Songs' and the other reading 'Mencius.' Recently, I added another one, a girl, who is reading 'The Book of Filial Piety.' I don't even teach mathematics, not because I don't want to, but because they don't want to learn it."

"I really didn't expect you to be teaching these kinds of books..."

"Their fathers want them to study these. I am just someone else, so I have no choice. These mundane matters are nothing. As long as it's casual..."

His face had turned completely red, indicating he was quite drunk, but his gaze became downcast. I sighed lightly and found myself at a loss for words. There was a commotion on the stairs as a few customers rushed up. In the lead was a short man with a bloated round face, followed by another man with prominent features, including a red nose. More people followed, causing the stairs to tremble. I glanced at Lu Weifu, and he happened to be looking at me. I called the waiter to settle the bill.

"Can you support yourself with this?" I asked as I prepared to leave.

"Yes. I have twenty yuan each month, which barely covers my expenses."

"So, what are your plans for the future?"

"The future? I don't know. Do you think we have anything desirable in mind for that time? I don't know anything now. I don't even know what tomorrow holds, not even the next minute..."

The waiter brought the bill and handed it to me. He no longer displayed the initial humility, merely giving me a glance before lighting a cigarette and allowing me to pay the bill.

We walked out of the shop together, his hotel being in the opposite direction of mine. We bid farewell at the doorstep. I walked alone towards my hotel, feeling the cold wind and snowflakes hitting my face, which strangely invigorated me. As dusk settled, the sky, buildings, and streets were all intertwined in the intricate, snow-covered web of pure white.

February 16, 1924.

SOAP

Mrs. Siming, carrying her 8-year-old daughter Xiuer, was pasting paper tablets in the slanting afternoon sunlight, with her back to the north window. Suddenly, she heard heavy and slow footsteps on straw sandals, knowing that Siming had entered the room. She didn't look at him, just continued pasting the paper tablets. But the sound of the straw sandals grew louder and closer, until it finally stopped by her side. Unable to resist, she turned her eyes and saw Siming standing right in front of her, vigorously digging into the pocket behind the front flap of his robe.

After a struggle, he finally managed to pull out his hand, holding a small rectangular package, green in color. He handed it directly to Mrs. Siming. As soon as she took it, a strange fragrance, resembling olives but not quite, wafted into her nose. She also noticed a dazzling golden seal and intricate patterns on the green wrapping paper. Xiuer immediately jumped over, wanting to take a look, but Mrs. Siming quickly pushed her away.

"Went to the market?" she asked while examining the package.

"Mm-hmm," he replied, his eyes fixed on the package in her hand.

Thus, the green package was opened. Inside, there was another thin layer of green paper. When she peeled back the thin paper, the true object was revealed. It was smooth and firm, also green in color, with delicate patterns on it. The thin paper, which had turned out to be a pale beige, exuded an even stronger fragrance, resembling olives but not quite.

"Oh, this is truly excellent soap," she said, holding the green item under her nose like a child, sniffing it.

"Mm-hmm, from now on, you should use this..." he said.

As she saw him speaking these words, her gaze fell on her neck, and she felt a warmth spreading across her face below her cheekbones. Sometimes, she accidentally touched her neck, especially behind her ears, and she always felt some roughness on her fingertips. She had known for a long time that it was accumulated dirt from years gone by, but it had never bothered her much. Now, under his gaze, facing this green, fragrant foreign soap, her face couldn't help but grow warm, and the warmth spread to her ears immediately. She decided that after dinner, she would use this soap and wash herself thoroughly.

"Some places can't be cleaned properly with just soapberries," she said to herself.

"Mom, give it to me!" Xiuer reached out to grab the green paper; her younger daughter, Zhaoer, who had been playing outside, also ran over. Mrs. Siming quickly pushed them away, wrapped the thin paper back around the soap, and rewrapped it with the green paper. She leaned over and placed it on the highest shelf of the washstand, took a look, and then resumed pasting the paper tablets.

"Xuecheng!" Siming remembered something and suddenly called out, elongating his voice, as he sat down on a high-backed chair opposite her.

"Xuecheng!" she joined in calling out.

She paused in pasting the paper tablets and listened, but there was no response. Seeing him anxiously waiting with his head raised, she couldn't help but feel apologetic. She made an effort to raise her voice and called sharply:

"Qian'er!"

This call seemed to be effective, as the sound of leather shoes gradually approached. Before long, Qian'er was standing in front of her, wearing only a short shirt, her plump round face shiny with sweat.

"What are you doing? Why didn't you hear Dad calling?" she reproached her.

"I was just practicing Bagua Fist..." Qian'er immediately turned and faced Siming, standing straight and looking at him, as if to ask what was the matter.

"Xuecheng, I want to ask you, what does 'evil woman' mean?"

"'Evil woman'?... Isn't that a 'very fierce woman'?" he replied.

"Nonsense! Ridiculous!" Siming suddenly became angry. "Am I a 'woman'!?"

Xuecheng took two steps back in fright and stood even straighter.

Although he sometimes felt that his walking resembled that of an actor on stage, he had never considered himself a woman. He knew he had answered incorrectly.

"'Evil woman' means 'very cruel woman,' I don't understand. I have to ask you? - This is not Chinese, it's the enemy's language, I'm telling you. What does it mean, do you understand?"

"I... I don't understand," Xuecheng became even more uneasy.

"Ha! I spent money to send you to school, and you don't even understand this little thing. It's a shame that your school boasts about 'equal emphasis on oral and written skills,' but it teaches you nothing. The person who speaks this foreign language is at most fourteen or fifteen years old, even younger than you, and they can already blabber away, but you can't even grasp the meaning. And you have the audacity to say 'I don't understand'! - Now go and find out for me!"

Xuecheng responded with a respectful "Yes" from his throat and left.

"This is truly unacceptable," after a while, Siming said generously. "Today's students... In fact, during the reign of Emperor Guangxu, I was the one advocating for the establishment of schools. But who would have expected that the flaws in the education system would be so serious: talking about liberation and freedom, without practical knowledge, just nonsense. As for Xuecheng, a considerable amount of money was spent on his education, all in vain. It was quite a feat to get him into a modern school with a combination of Chinese and Western education, emphasizing both Chinese and English. You would think that would be enough, but after a year of studying, he doesn't even understand 'evil woman.' He's probably still stuck in rote learning. Ha! What kind of school is this? What has it produced? I can say it outright: they should all be shut down!"

"Yes, it would be better to shut them all down," Mrs. Siming pasted the paper tablets sympathetically.

"Xiuer and the others don't need to go to school either. 'Girls, why bother with books?' Old Master Jiu said that when he was opposing girls' education, and I criticized him. But now, it seems that the words of the elderly are indeed correct. Think about it, women walking in the streets in bursts, it's already quite indecent, yet they still want to cut their hair. What I despise the most are those female students who cut their hair. I can say it outright, soldiers and bandits can be somewhat forgiven, but it's them who are causing turmoil in the world. They should be dealt with strictly..."

"Yes, it's not enough for men to become monks. Now women are trying to become nuns."

"Xuecheng!"

Xuecheng entered briskly, holding a small but thick book with golden edges, and presented it to Siming, pointing to a certain section.

"This is somewhat similar. This..."

When Siming took a look at it, he realized it was a dictionary, but the text was very small and printed horizontally. He furrowed his brows, held it up to the window, squinted his eyes, and read aloud the line that Xuecheng pointed to:

"'The name of the society founded in the 18th century by the Freemasons.' Hmm, that's not right. How is this pronounced?" He pointed to the word "guizi" (foreigner) in front and asked.

"Oddfellows."

"No, no, that's not it." Siming grew angry again. "Let me tell you: that's a curse, an insult directed at people like me. Understand? Go and find out!"

Xuecheng glanced at him but didn't move.

"What kind of nonsense is this? You should explain it clearly first so that he knows how to search properly." Siming saw Xuecheng's hesitation and felt sorry for him, so she tried to pacify her husband while expressing her dissatisfaction.

"It's when I was buying soap at Guangrunxiang on the main street," Siming took a deep breath and turned to face her as he spoke. "There were three students buying things in the shop. Naturally, I didn't want to appear stingy in front of them. I looked at six or seven items, all priced over four cents, so I didn't buy them. The ones priced at one cent or one yuan were too poor in quality and lacked fragrance. I thought the ones in the middle were better, so I chose the green one for two yuan and four fen. The shop assistant was already a snobbish fellow with eyes growing out of his forehead, constantly pursing his dog-like mouth. What infuriated me was that those students, the mischievous brats, were winking and speaking gibberish, laughing at me. Later, when I wanted to open it and take a look before paying, the soap was wrapped in foreign paper. How could I determine its quality without opening it? But that snobbish shop assistant not only refused, he was also unreasonably stubborn and said a lot of hateful nonsense, while the brats echoed and laughed. The smallest one among them said it, and when they all looked at me, they burst into laughter. It's clear that it must be an insult." He then turned to Xuecheng and said, "Just search in the 'insult' category!"

Xuecheng responded with a respectful "Yes" from his throat and left.

"They keep shouting about 'new culture, new culture,' but it has deteriorated to this point. Isn't it enough?" Siming fixed his gaze on the ceiling beam and continued speaking to himself. "The students have no morality, and society has no morality either. If we don't think of a way to save it, China is truly doomed. Can you imagine how lamentable that is?"

"What?" she casually asked, not surprised.

"A filial daughter," he turned to her in an instant and said solemnly. "Right on the main street, there were two beggars. One was a girl, probably around eighteen or nineteen years old. Actually, at that age, begging is very inappropriate, but she still begged. She sat under the eaves of a cloth shop with an old woman in her sixties or seventies, with white hair and blind eyes, begging for alms. Everyone said she was a filial daughter, and the old woman was her grandmother. Whatever she managed to beg, she would offer it all to her grandmother to eat, willingly going hungry herself. But for such a filial daughter, would anyone be willing to give alms?" He fixed his gaze on her, as if testing her insight.

She didn't answer, only kept her eyes fixed on him, seemingly waiting for him to explain.

"Hmm, no," he finally answered himself. "I watched for a long time and only saw one person give a penny; the rest formed a big circle and made fun of them. There were even two rascals who shamelessly said, 'Ah Fa, don't look at this dirty stuff. Just buy two bars of soap and wash yourself all over, it'll be fine!' Now, what do you think of that?"

"Hmm," she lowered her head. After a while, she lazily asked, "Did you give them any money?"

"Me? No. It would be embarrassing to give just one or two coins. It's not ordinary begging, after all, so I thought..."

"Hmm," she didn't wait for him to finish speaking. Slowly, she stood up and walked to the kitchen. The dim light made everything appear denser, and it was already dinner time.

Siming also stood up and walked out of the courtyard. The sky was brighter than inside the house, and Xuecheng was practicing Baguazhang in the corner of the wall. It was his "court training," an economical method he had been practicing for nearly half a year, making use of the transitional time between day and night. Siming nodded slightly in approval and then paced back and forth in the empty courtyard with his hands behind his back. Before long, the only potted plant, a broad-leaved evergreen, disappeared into the darkness, and tiny stars flickered amidst the white clouds like scattered cotton. The night began from there. At this moment, Siming couldn't help but feel inspired, as if he was about to accomplish something significant and declare war on the surrounding unruly students and the corrupt society. His spirit gradually became bold, his steps wider, and the sound of his cloth shoes grew louder, startling the mother hen and chicks that had long since fallen asleep in their coop, making them chirp and cluck.

There was light in the hall, like the beacon calling for dinner. The family members gathered around the central table. The lamp hung from below, and at the head of the table sat Siming, with his round face resembling Xuecheng's, but with a thin mustache. In the steam of the dishes, he occupied one side, resembling the deity in a temple. On the left sat Siming's wife with Zhaor, and on the right sat Xuecheng and Xiuer. The sound of utensils clinking was like the pitter-patter of raindrops, and although no one spoke, it was a lively dinner.

Zhaor had already finished her rice and the soup spilled across half the table. Siming widened his eyes as much as possible, staring at her as if she were about to cry. He then withdrew his gaze, picked up his chopsticks, and tried to pick up the vegetable dish he had set his eyes on earlier. But the dish had disappeared. He glanced left and right and saw Xuecheng had just stuffed it into his large mouth. So, Siming reluctantly ate a few leaves of yellow vegetables.

"Xuecheng," he looked at his face and said, "Did you find that phrase?"

"That phrase? No, not yet."

"Hmm, you see, you have no knowledge, no understanding of reason, you only know how to eat! Learn from that filial daughter, even as a beggar, she is devoted to her grandmother and willingly goes hungry. But you students, you have no knowledge of such things, you act recklessly, and in the future, you'll end up like those rascals..."

"I thought of one phrase, but I'm not sure if it's the right one. Maybe they were saying 'old fool'."

"Oh, yes! That's it! They were saying something like 'evil old fool'. What does it mean? You are part of their group: you know."

"Meaning... I don't quite understand."

"Nonsense! You're hiding it from me. You're all rotten!"

"The heavens won't strike someone who's eating. Why are you so irritable today? You're even scolding and cursing during dinner. What do those kids know?" Siming's wife suddenly interjected.

"What?" Siming was about to say something, but when he turned his head, he saw that her sunken cheeks had puffed up, and her complexion had changed. Her triangular eyes emitted a terrifying light. He quickly changed his tone and said, "I'm not irritable. I just want Xuecheng to be more sensible."

"He doesn't understand what's in your heart," she said, getting even more annoyed. "If he were sensible, he would have lit a lantern and gone to find that filial daughter already. Fortunately, you've already bought a bar of soap for her here. You just need to buy one more..."

"Nonsense! Those words were spoken by that rascal."

"It's not necessarily so. Just buy one more and let her wash herself thoroughly. Once she's provided for, everything will be peaceful in the world."

"What does that have to do with anything? I mentioned it because I remembered that you don't have any soap..."

"How is it irrelevant? You bought it specifically for the filial daughter. Go and wash yourself thoroughly. I don't deserve it, I don't want it, I don't want to bask in the glory of the filial daughter."

"What kind of talk is this? You women..." Siming hesitated, sweat oozing from his face as if he had been practicing Baguazhang like Xuecheng, but it was probably because he had eaten hot food.

"What about us women? We women are much better than you men. You men either curse at eighteen or nineteen-year-old female students or praise eighteen or nineteen-year-old female beggars. None of you have good intentions. 'Wash yourself thoroughly' is simply shameless!"

"Haven't I already said? It was a rascal..."

"Father!" A loud cry suddenly came from outside.

"Dao Weng? I'm coming!" Siming knew it was the loud and well-known He Dao Tong, so he happily and cheerfully said, "Xuecheng, quickly light the lamp and guide Uncle He to the study!"

Xuecheng lit a candle and led Dao Tong into the west wing, followed by Bu Wei Yuan.

"Apologies for the late reception," Siming said as he came out, still chewing his food, and bowed. "Shall we have a casual meal in the study?"

"We've missed it already," Wei Yuan stepped forward, also bowing, and said. "We came overnight just for the topic of the 18th

Annual Writing Competition of the Moving Winds Literary Society. Isn't tomorrow the 'seventh'?"

"Oh! Today is the sixteenth?" Siming said in realization.

"You see, how muddled!" Dao Tong shouted loudly.

"So, it has to be sent to the newspaper office overnight and be published tomorrow without fail."

"I've already drafted the title. What do you think, can we use it or not?" Dao Tong said, digging out a piece of paper from his handkerchief and handing it to him.

Siming paced over to the candlestick, unfolded the paper, and read it word by word:

"'Respectfully proposing a nationwide joint appeal to Your Excellency, the President, to issue a special decree emphasizing the veneration of the Bible and the revival of the essence of Meng Mu's teachings to preserve the cultural heritage of the nation.' - Very good, excellent. But isn't it too long?"

"It doesn't matter!" Dao Tong said loudly. "I've done the calculations, and there's no need for additional advertising fees. But what about the poem title?"

"The poem title?" Siming suddenly assumed a respectful posture. "I have one here: 'The Filial Daughter's Deeds.' It's based on real events and should commend her. Today, I was on the street..."

"Oh, no. That won't work." Wei Yuan quickly shook her head and interrupted him. "I saw that too. She's probably an 'outsider.' I don't understand her language, and she doesn't understand mine. I don't know where she's from. Everyone says she's a filial daughter, but when I asked her if she could write poetry, she shook her head. It would have been nice if she could."

"However, loyalty and filial piety are important virtues. Even if she can't write poetry, we can make do..."

"But it's not like that, who knows!" Wei Yuan spread her palms and rushed over to Siming, shaking and pushing, trying to persuade him. "She should be able to write poetry, and it would be interesting."

"We," Siming pushed him away, "will use this title, along with an explanation, and publish it in the newspaper. First, it can commend her, and second, it can criticize society. What kind of society is it now? I observed from the sidelines for a long time and didn't see anyone giving her a penny. Isn't that heartless..."

"Oh, my goodness, Siming!" Wei Yuan rushed over again. "You're simply 'insulting the monk in front of the bald head.' I didn't give her money either because I happened to not have any with me at that time."

"Don't take it to heart, Wei Yuan." Siming pushed him away again. "You were naturally outside and had a different perspective. Listen to me: There was a large crowd around them, showing no respect, just making fun. There were even two rascals, who were even more shameless. One of them actually said, 'Ah Fa, go buy two bars of soap and wash yourself thoroughly, it would be great.' Just think about it..."

"Hahaha! Two bars of soap!" Dao Tong's loud laughter suddenly erupted, ringing in people's ears. "You buy them, hahaha, hahaha!"

"Dao Tong, Dao Tong, don't make such a fuss." Siming was startled and said anxiously.

"Gok gok, hahaha!"

"Dao Tong!" Siming's face turned serious. "We're discussing serious matters, why are you only fooling around and making people dizzy? Listen, we'll immediately send these two titles to the newspaper office and demand that they be published tomorrow without fail. We can only rely on the two of you for this task."

"That's fine, of course," Wei Yuan readily agreed.

"Hehe, wash, gok... sigh..."

"Dao Tong!!!" Siming angrily shouted.

With this reprimand, Dao Tong stopped laughing. They prepared the explanation, which Wei Yuan transcribed on a letter, and then ran off to the newspaper office with Dao Tong. Siming held the candlestick and saw them off at the door. When he returned to the outer room of the hall, he felt somewhat uneasy. After a brief hesitation, he finally stepped over the threshold. As soon as he entered, he saw the small rectangular package of green soap placed in the middle of the table. The golden seal in the center of the package gleamed under the light, surrounded by delicate patterns.

Xiu'er and Zhao'er were squatting and playing on the floor under the table, while Xuecheng sat to the right, looking up words in the dictionary. Finally, in the shadow farthest from the light, he spotted Mrs. Si, with a stiff expression on her face, showing neither joy nor anger, her eyes not focused on anything.

"Gok gok, shameless... shameless..."

Siming faintly heard Xiu'er say behind him. When he turned to look, there was no movement, only Zhao'er was using her fingers to scratch her own face.

He felt restless and extinguished the candle, strolling out of the courtyard. He paced back and forth, and accidentally, the mother hen and the chicks started clucking again. He immediately lightened his footsteps and walked farther away. After a while, the light from the hall moved into the bedroom. He saw the moonlight on the ground, as if it were covered in seamless white gauze, and the moon, like a jade plate, was now hidden among the white clouds, showing no signs of a blemish.

He felt a sense of sadness, as if he, like the filial daughter, had become a "bereaved citizen," lonely and destitute. He slept very late that night.

But by the next morning, the soap had been accepted. On this day, he woke up later than usual and saw her already bent over the washstand, wiping her neck. The soap foam piled high behind her ears, resembling bubbles on a crab's mouth, a far cry from the thin layer of foam when she used soap nuts before. From then on, Mrs. Si always carried a subtle and indescribable scent, similar to olives but not quite. It lasted for nearly half a year before suddenly changing, and everyone who caught a whiff of it said it seemed like sandalwood.

March 22, 1924.

DRAGON BOAT FESTIVAL

Recently, Fang Xuanchuo has been fond of saying "almost" as if it has become his "catchphrase." Not only does he say it, but it has also taken root in his mind. Initially, he would say "they're all the same," but later, feeling that it lacked stability, he changed it to "almost" and has been using it ever since.

Since he discovered this ordinary phrase, it has brought about many new reflections and comforts for him. For example, when he sees the older generation exerting pressure on the younger generation, he used to feel indignant at first. But now, he thinks to himself that when these young people have children and grandchildren, they will probably adopt the same attitude, so he no longer feels any resentment. Similarly, when he sees a soldier hitting a rickshaw puller, he used to feel angry at first. But now, he thinks to himself that if the rickshaw puller became a soldier and the soldier became a rickshaw puller, they would probably act in the same way, so he no longer takes offense. At times, he wonders if this line of thinking is just an intentional escape route he has created out of a lack of courage to fight against an unjust society. It is akin to having a "moral ambiguity" and is far from being a desirable solution. However, this viewpoint continues to grow in his mind.

The first time he publicly expressed this "almost" statement was in the lecture hall of Beijing Shoushan School. It was probably during a discussion about historical events when he mentioned that "people of the past and present are not far apart" and talked about the "similarities in human nature." Eventually, he touched upon students and bureaucrats, launching into a discussion:

"Nowadays, it's fashionable in society to criticize bureaucrats, and students are particularly adept at it. However, bureaucrats are not a special race born from the heavens; they are just commoners turned officials. There are many officials who come from a student background now, so what's the difference between them and the old bureaucrats? 'If you switch places, it's all the same.' There is not much difference in their thoughts, speech, or actions... Even many initiatives started by student organizations have inevitably fallen into corruption and most of them have fizzled out. It's almost the same. But this is what we should worry about for China's future..."

Among the twenty or so listeners in the lecture hall, some felt melancholic, perhaps thinking that what he said was true. Some felt outraged, possibly considering it an insult to the sacred youth. However, a few smiled at him, probably believing that he was defending himself because Fang Xuanchuo himself is also a bureaucrat.

But in reality, it's all wrong. It's just his new source of discontentment, and even though he feels discontented, it's merely a passive theory. He himself doesn't know whether it's because he's lazy or useless, but he always sees himself as someone who refuses to make any effort and is very content with staying in his own lane. He always keeps silent as long as his position is not threatened; even when the teachers' salaries have been overdue for nearly half a year, he never speaks up as long as he has his official income to support him. Not only does he not speak up, but when the teachers collectively demand their wages, he secretly thinks they are being too demanding and making too much noise. It was only when he heard his colleagues mocking them excessively that he felt a slight sense of sympathy. Then, he had a thought that perhaps it was because he himself was short of money, and it had nothing to do with other officials who were not also teachers. And so, he let it go.

Although he is also short of money, he has never joined the teachers' group, and when they decided to boycott classes, he did not stop attending classes. When the government said, "We will only pay if you attend classes," he slightly resented their way of treating them like monkeys playing with fruits. When a prominent educator said, "Teachers carrying school bags in one hand and demanding money with the other is not noble," he formally complained to his wife.

"Hey, why are there only two dishes?" During dinner on the day of the "not noble" remark, he looked at the food and said.

They hadn't received a new education, and his wife had no

formal title or nickname, so there was no specific way to address her. According to tradition, he could call her "Mrs.," but he didn't want to be too old-fashioned, so he came up with the word "Hey." His wife didn't even have a "Hey" for him; as long as she faced him when speaking, according to customary law, he knew she was addressing him.

"But we used up all the one-and-a-half months' worth of money we received last month... Even yesterday's rice was only obtained on credit with great difficulty," she stood by the table, facing him as she spoke.

"You see, they say it's despicable to ask for a salary as a teacher. These people don't seem to understand even the most basic things, like how people need to eat, rice is needed for meals, and rice requires money to buy... "

"Exactly. Without money, how can we buy rice? And without rice, how can we cook..."

His cheeks puffed up as if he was annoyed that her answer was "almost" in line with his argument, as if he was just echoing his own words. Then he turned his head to the other side, a signal according to customary law that the discussion was over.

On the day when the bleak wind and cold rain arrived, the teachers, after being beaten by the national army in the muddy ground in front of Xinhuamen for demanding their unpaid salaries, surprisingly received a small portion of their wages. Without lifting a finger, Fang Xuancho effortlessly collected the money, repaid some old debts, but still fell short of a large sum because his official salary was also significantly overdue. At that time, even the upright officials began to believe that the wages should not be left unpaid, especially for teachers like Fang Xuancho, who was also sympathetic to the academic community. So when everyone advocated for the continuation of the boycott, although he did not attend the meetings, he wholeheartedly respected and adhered to the collective decision.

However, the government unexpectedly paid the salaries, and schools resumed classes. But in the preceding days, there were always students who submitted a document to the government stating, "If teachers don't teach, then don't pay their overdue salaries." Although this had no effect, it reminded Fang Xuancho of the government's previous statement, "We will only pay if classes are held." The shadow of "almost" flickered before his eyes again and did not disappear. As a result, he publicly expressed it in the lecture hall.

Therefore, it can be seen that if we elaborate on the concept of "almost," it can naturally be interpreted as a form of discontent driven by personal motives, but it cannot be said that it is solely an excuse for being an official. It's just that in such situations, he often liked to bring up questions about the future fate of China. Carelessly, he even considered himself a patriot: people always suffer from a lack of "self-awareness."

However, the fact of "almost" happened again. Although the government initially ignored the troublesome teachers, they later extended their indifference to the inconsequential officials as well. The debts kept piling up, eventually forcing some previously disdainful officials, who had demanded wages, to become prominent figures in the wage-seeking assembly. Only a few newspapers expressed disdain and mockery towards them. Fang Xuancho was not surprised at all and didn't mind because, based on his "almost" theory, he knew that these were just the result of news reporters still having an inkling of criticism. In case the government or wealthy individuals cut off their subsidies, most likely they would also convene such assemblies.

Since he had shown sympathy for the teachers' wage demands, it was natural for him to support his colleagues' salary demands as well. However, he continued to sit comfortably in the yamen and, as usual, did not join the debt collection efforts. As for those who doubted his aloofness, it was simply a misunderstanding. He claimed that throughout his life, people had always come to him for debts, and he had never gone to others to collect debts, so this was not his expertise. Moreover, he was most afraid of encountering individuals who held economic power. While these people may appear amiable when they lost their authority and preached Buddhist studies with the book "Mahayana Mahaparinirvana Sutra" in hand, when they were still in power, they always wore the face of Yama, treating others as servants and believing they had the power of life and death over poor fellows like him. Because of this, he dared not meet them and was unwilling to meet them. Although sometimes he himself felt that this temperament was haughty, he often suspected that it was actually a lack of ability.

After much searching and negotiation, everyone managed to scrape by, one section at a time. However, compared to before, Fang Xuancho was in an extremely dire situation. Therefore, it was needless to say that the servants he employed and the shops he dealt with were affected. Even Fang's wife gradually lost respect for him. Just by observing her recent lack of agreement, frequent expression of original opinions, and some abrupt behavior, he could understand. On the morning of the fourth day of the fifth lunar month, when he returned home, she thrust a stack of bills in front of his nose, something that had never happened before.

"We need a total of 180 yuan to cover expenses... Did you receive it?" She didn't look at him while speaking.

"Hmph, I won't be an official tomorrow. I received the check for the money, but the representatives of the wage-seeking assembly refused to distribute it. At first, they said they wouldn't give it to those who didn't attend, and later they said we had to personally go to them to collect it. Once they got hold of the checks today, they turned into Yama's face. I'm truly afraid to see them... I don't want the money, and I won't be an official anymore. It's too humiliating..."

Fang's wife was somewhat taken aback by this rare display of indignation but remained calm.

"I think it's better to go and collect it personally. What's the big deal?" She looked at his face and said.

"I won't go! This is our salary, not a reward. It should be delivered by the accounting department as usual."

"But what if they don't deliver it... Oh, I forgot to mention last night, the children said that the school has already reminded several times about the tuition fees, saying that if we don't pay..."

"Nonsense! They don't pay me for my work as a teacher, but they want money for our son to study a few books?"

She felt that he was no longer concerned about reason and seemed to vent his frustration as if he were the school principal. It wasn't worth engaging, so she stopped speaking.

The two of them silently ate their lunch. After thinking for a while, he regretfully went out again.

As usual, in recent years, on the eve of festivals or holidays, he always had to return home at midnight. While walking, he reached into his pocket and shouted loudly, "Hey, I've received it!" Then he handed a stack of brand-new banknotes to her with a proud expression on his face. Unexpectedly, on the fourth day, he broke this tradition and returned home before 7 o'clock. Fang's wife was very surprised and suspicious, thinking that he had actually resigned from his job. However, she secretly observed his face but didn't notice any extraordinary expression of misfortune.

"What happened?... So early?..." She asked, fixing her gaze on him.

"It couldn't be issued, I couldn't collect it. The bank has already closed, and we have to wait until the morning of the eighth day."

"Collect it personally?" She asked anxiously.

"The personal collection option has been canceled, I heard it will still be distributed by the accounting department. But the bank has closed today and will rest for three days. We have to wait until the morning of the eighth day." He sat down, looked at the ground, took a sip of tea, and then slowly spoke again. "Fortunately, there are no issues at the yamen anymore. We should have the money by the eighth day... It's really troublesome to borrow money from unrelated relatives and friends. In the afternoon, I reluctantly went to find Jin Yongsheng. After talking for a while, he initially praised me for not demanding wages and refusing to collect it personally, saying it was very noble and the right thing to do. But as soon as he learned that I wanted to borrow fifty yuan from him, it was as if I had stuffed a handful of salt in his mouth. Every wrinkle on his face appeared, and he started talking about how he couldn't afford the rent, how his business was losing money, and how it was nothing to collect the payment in front of colleagues. He immediately sent me away."

"In such an urgent festival, who would be willing to lend money?" Fang's wife said calmly, without much emotion.

Fang Xuanchuo lowered his head, feeling that it was not surprising, especially since he and Jin Yongsheng were already distant. He then remembered what happened during the previous year's holiday season. At that time, a fellow villager came to borrow ten yuan. He had already received the payment voucher from the yamen, but fearing that the person might not repay the money in the future, he put on a hesitant expression and said that since he couldn't collect his salary from the yamen and the school wasn't paying either, he really couldn't help and sent him away empty-handed. Although he didn't see what expression he had on his face, at this moment, he felt very uneasy, his lips moved slightly, and he shook his head.

However, not long after, he suddenly realized something and gave an order: he told the servant to immediately go to the street and buy a bottle of Lianhua Bai on credit. He knew that the shopkeeper would want to settle the account tomorrow, so they wouldn't dare not provide it on credit. If they didn't provide it on credit, they wouldn't receive a single penny tomorrow, which was the punishment they deserved.

They managed to get the Lianhua Bai on credit. He drank two cups, and a flush appeared on his pale face. After finishing the meal, he became quite happy. He lit a large Haidemen cigarette and grabbed a copy of "Essays" from the table, intending to read it while lying on the bed.

"Well, how should we deal with the shopkeeper tomorrow?" Fang's wife caught up, stood in front of the bed, and looked at his face.

"The shopkeeper?... Tell them to come on the second half of the eighth day."

"I can't say that. They won't believe it and won't agree."

"What's there not to believe? They can ask around. No one in the entire yamen has received it. Everyone will get it on the eighth day!" He gestured with his second finger, drawing a semicircle in the air, and Fang's wife followed the gesture, also looking at a semicircle. Then she saw his hand flipping open the "Essays."

Seeing that he was being unreasonable beyond imagination, Fang's wife temporarily couldn't find a way to respond.

"I think this situation can't continue. We will have to think of something, do something else in the future..." She finally found another path to explore.

"What else can I do? 'I'm not a scribe to transcribe, nor a firefighter to save the fire.' What else can I do?" he replied.

"Didn't you write articles for the bookstores in Shanghai?"

"The bookstores in Shanghai? They count the characters one by one when buying manuscripts. Even spaces aren't included. Look at the prose poems I wrote there. How much empty space is there? It's probably only worth three hundred coins per book. And the copyright royalties haven't been paid for six months. 'Distant water cannot put out a nearby fire.' Who has the patience for that?"

"So, what about the newspaper office here?"

"The newspaper office? Even in this big newspaper office, with the favor of a student working as an editor there, a thousand words would only earn me a few coins. Even if I worked from morning till night, could I support all of you? Besides, I don't have that many articles in me."

"So, what do we do after the festival?"

"After the festival?... I'll still continue with my official duties. When the shopkeepers come for money tomorrow, just tell them the afternoon of the eighth."

He was about to read "Essays" again. Fang's wife was afraid of missing the opportunity and hurriedly said with hesitation, "I was thinking, after the festival, on the eighth, we... why don't we buy a lottery ticket..."

"Nonsense! How can you say something so uneducated..."

At that moment, he suddenly remembered what happened after being sent away by Jin Yongsheng. At that time, he walked through Daoxiang Village in a daze and saw many big words on the advertisement outside the shop, saying, "First prize, several tens of thousands of yuan." It seemed to stir something in his heart, perhaps slowing down his footsteps. However, it seemed that he walked away resolutely, maybe because he couldn't bear to part with the six jiao coins left in his wallet. His expression changed, and Fang's wife thought he was upset about her uneducated remark, so she quickly stepped back and didn't finish her sentence. Fang Xuanchuo also didn't finish his sentence, he stretched his waist, and mumbled as he read "Essays".

June 1922.

THE SKY MENDER

CHAPTER 1

Nüwa suddenly woke up.

It seemed as though she had awakened from a dream, but she couldn't remember what dream it was. She felt regretful, sensing something lacking and something excessive. The stirring gentle breeze blew, spreading her strength throughout the universe.

She rubbed her eyes.

In the pink sky, numerous winding stone-green clouds drifted, with stars flickering behind them. In the blood-red clouds on the horizon, a radiant sun shone like a flowing golden sphere wrapped in primordial lava. On the other side, there was a moon as cold and white as pig iron. Yet, she paid no attention to who was going down or who was coming up.

The ground was tenderly green, and even the evergreen pines and cypresses appeared especially delicate. Peach blossoms and large patches of multicolored flowers were vividly visible nearby, but in the distance, they became a colorful mist.

"Ah, I have never been so bored!" she thought and suddenly stood up, raising her perfectly rounded and energetic arm, stretching and yawning. The sky immediately lost its color and transformed into a mystical fleshy red, temporarily concealing her whereabouts.

Amidst this fleshy red world, she walked to the seashore, her entire body's curves dissolving into the faint rosy glow of the sea until only a central part remained dense and pure white. The waves were astonished, undulating in an orderly manner, but the spray splashed onto her body. This pure white silhouette trembled in the seawater, as if it were dispersing in all directions. However, she herself did not see it, only involuntarily kneeling down and scooping up the muddy water in her hands, then kneading it a few times until something small, similar to herself, appeared in her hands.

"Ah, ah!" She naturally believed she had created it, but she also doubted that this thing, like a sweet potato, had originally existed in the soil. This filled her with astonishment.

However, this astonishment delighted her, and with unprecedented courage and joy, she continued her endeavor, breathing and sweating...

"Nga! Nga!" Those little things started to make noise.

"Ah, ah!" She was startled again, feeling as if something was dispersing from every pore of her body. As a result, the ground was covered in milky white smoke, and she regained her composure. The little things also fell silent.

"Akon, Agon!" Something said to her.

"Ah, ah, adorable babies." She fixed her gaze on them and extended her muddy fingers to poke their chubby faces.

"Uvu, Ahaha!" They laughed. It was the first time she had seen laughter in the heavens and earth, and she found herself laughing uncontrollably, unable to close her lips.

While caressing them, she continued her work, and the things being made circled around her. But gradually, they moved further away, spoke more, and she couldn't understand anymore. She only felt her ears filled with noisy clamor, which made her feel somewhat dizzy.

In the midst of prolonged joy, she was already weary. She had almost exhausted her breath and sweat, and on top of that, she felt dizzy. Her vision became blurry, and her cheeks grew warm. She didn't care anymore and became impatient. However, she continued to work unconsciously.

Eventually, the soreness in her waist and legs forced her to stand up, leaning against a smooth mountain. Looking up, the sky was filled with fish-scale-like white clouds, while below was a densely green expanse. She didn't know why, but she felt dissatisfied with her surroundings, becoming agitated and reaching out her hand. Without thinking, she pulled out a wisteria vine that stretched from the mountain to the sky. It bloomed with indescribably large purple flowers in clusters. With a swing of her hand, the vine lay horizontally on the ground, scattering petals of purple and white all over.

She then waved her hand, causing the wisteria vine to flip in the mud and water, splashing muddy water in the process. When it landed on the ground, it turned into many small things similar to what she had made before, but most of them had dull and silly expressions, somewhat annoying. However, she had no time to pay attention to such matters. It was simply entertaining and irritating. With mischievousness, she swung her hand faster and faster, causing the vine to roll on the ground, dragging mud and water like a red-hot boiling snake. Mud splattered from the vine like a torrential rain, turning into wailing little things in the air, crawling and scattering all over the ground.

She was on the verge of losing consciousness, swinging even harder. But not only her waist and legs were in pain, even her two arms had become weak. She couldn't help but squat down, leaning her head against the high mountain, with her jet-black hair resting on the mountaintop. After taking a breath and sighing, she closed her eyes. The wisteria vine slipped from her hands and lazily lay on the ground, as if exhausted.

CHAPTER 2

Boom!!! In the midst of this earth-shattering sound, Nüwa suddenly woke up and swiftly slid down to the southeast. She extended her foot to step on something, but couldn't find anything to tread on. Quickly, she reached out and grabbed hold of a mountain peak, preventing herself from sliding further downward.

But she felt water and sand rolling and splashing from behind onto her head and around her. She turned her head slightly and ended up taking a mouthful of water and filling both of her ears. She quickly lowered her head and saw the ground shaking incessantly. Fortunately, the shaking seemed to calm down. She shifted backward and stabilized her body, then wiped the water off her forehead and around her eyes, trying to see the situation clearly.

The situation was quite unclear, with waterfalls flowing everywhere, perhaps the sea. There were several sharp waves rising in some places. She could only wait in a daze.

But finally, there was a great calm. The large waves were only as high as the mountains used to be, revealing the rugged skeletal structure of the land. Nüwa was looking towards the sea when she saw several mountains rushing towards her, swirling amidst the waves. She was afraid that these mountains would collide with her feet, so she reached out and caught them, peering into the mountain hollows where many unseen things were still hidden.

She pulled her hand back, bringing the mountains closer to take a closer look. She noticed that the ground beside those things was in disarray, as if covered in gold and jade powder mixed with chewed pine and cypress leaves and fish flesh. Slowly, they began to lift their heads. Nüwa opened her round eyes, finally realizing that these were the small things she had created before, but now they had taken on strange forms and were wrapped in something. Some of them even had white fur growing on the lower half of their faces, looking like sharp white poplar leaves soaked in seawater.

"Ahh, ahh!" Nüwa exclaimed in surprise and fear, her skin covered in goosebumps as if pricked by thorns.

"Supreme Being, please save us..." one of them with white fur on the lower half of his face raised his head, intermittently vomiting while saying, "Save us... we are immortals in training. Unexpectedly, a catastrophe has occurred, and the heavens and earth are crumbling... Fortunately, we have encountered the Supreme Being... Please save our ant-like lives... and bestow us with immortal... immortal medicine..." As he finished speaking, he made a peculiar gesture with his head.

Nüwa was bewildered and could only ask, "What?"

Many of them started speaking, all vomiting while shouting, "Supreme Being, Supreme Being!" They all made similar gestures. Nüwa was annoyed by their disturbance and regretted pulling them up, causing this inexplicable trouble. She looked around helplessly and saw a group of giant tortoises playing on the sea's surface. Nüwa couldn't help but feel delighted and immediately placed those mountains on their backs, instructing, "Take me to a stable place!" The giant tortoises seemed to nod and moved away in groups. However, due to the excessive force used in the earlier pull, one of the faces with white fur fell from the mountain and couldn't catch up. It didn't know how to swim and could only lie on the shore, slapping itself. This made Nüwa feel sorry for it, but she didn't care because she didn't have time to deal with these matters.

Yi let out a sigh of relief, feeling somewhat lighter. When she turned her gaze to her surroundings, she noticed that the water had receded quite a bit, revealing vast stretches of earth and rocks. Many things were embedded in the cracks of the rocks, some stiff and motionless, while others were still moving. Yi caught sight of one of them staring blankly at her with wide eyes. It was covered in iron plates, and its expression seemed disappointed and afraid.

"What's going on here?" Yi casually asked.

"Alas, calamity has befallen us," the iron-clad creature lamented pitifully. "Zhuanxu betrayed us, and I, in retaliation, confronted the heavens, fighting in the outskirts. But the heavens did not bless my virtue, and my teacher turned against me..."

"What?" Yi had never heard such words before and was greatly surprised.

"My teacher turned against me, and I, in my desperation, struck my head against Mount Bu Zhou, breaking the pillar that supports the heavens. I fell to the ground, my life extinguished. Alas, it is indeed..."

"That's enough, I don't understand what you mean." Yi turned her face away, but then she saw another face, one that appeared happy and proud, also covered in iron plates.

"What's going on here?" Yi now realized that these little creatures could have such different faces, so she wanted to ask a different, more comprehensible question.

"The hearts of people have lost their ancient purity. Kanghui indeed had treacherous intentions, coveting the heavenly throne. I, in retaliation, confronted the heavens, fighting in the outskirts. The heavens did bless my virtue, and my teacher fought invincibly, vanquishing Kanghui at Mount Bu Zhou."

"What?" Yi still didn't quite understand.

"The hearts of people have lost their ancient purity..."

"That's enough, it's the same old story!" Yi became angry, her cheeks turning red all the way to her ears. She quickly turned her head away and continued searching. Finally, she saw something without iron plates, its body naked and bleeding from wounds, though it had a piece of tattered cloth around its waist. It was in the process of taking the torn cloth from another stiff creature's waist and hurriedly tying it around its own waist, but its expression remained calm.

Yi thought that this creature, unlike the ones covered in iron plates, might provide some clues, so she asked, "What's going on here?"

"What's going on?" it replied, lifting its head slightly.

"What about the commotion just now?"

"What about the commotion just now?"

"Was there a war?" Yi had no choice but to make her own guess.

"A war?" it asked in return.

Nüwa took a sharp breath and looked up at the sky. There was a large crack in the sky, deep and wide. Yi stood up and flicked it with her fingernail, but it made a dull sound, almost like the sound of a broken bowl. Furrowing her brow, Yi looked around and pondered for a while. Then she wrung out the water from her hair, separated it and draped it over her shoulders, and rallied herself to gather reeds and firewood. Yi had made up her mind to "fix it later."

From that day on, Yi piled up reeds day and night. The higher the pile, the thinner she became because the situation was not like before. The sky was skewed and cracked when she looked up, and the ground was dirty and dilapidated when she looked down. There was nothing pleasing to the eye.

When the reed pile reached the crack, Yi went to find some green stones. She had initially wanted to use pure green stones that matched the sky, but there weren't enough of them on the ground, and the mountains were reluctant to give them up. Sometimes she went to bustling places to find scraps, but she would be met with scorn, curses, or even have them snatched away, sometimes even biting her hand. So she had to resort to using white stones and, if not enough, she would add some red, yellow, and gray ones. Finally, she managed to fill the crack, and all it took was a spark, a melting, and the task was completed. However, Yi was exhausted, her head spinning, unable to continue.

"Ah, I've never been so bored before." Yi sat on a mountaintop, holding her head in her hands, panting heavily.

The great fire in the ancient forest of Kunlun Mountain was still not extinguished, and the western horizon was glowing red. Yi glanced to the west, determined to take a burning tree from there to ignite the reed pile. But just as she was about to reach out, she felt something pricking her toes.

Yi looked down and saw, as usual, the little things she had created before, but they were even more peculiar. They were covered in pieces of cloth, hanging from their bodies, with over a dozen pieces of cloth draped around their waists. Something unknown covered their heads, and on top was a small, black rectangular board. They held an object in their hands, which was what had pricked Yi's toes.

The one with the rectangular board happened to be standing between Nüwa's legs, looking up. As soon as they saw Yi's glance, they hurriedly handed over the small object. When Yi took it and looked at it, it was a smooth piece of green bamboo with two lines of black dots on it, much smaller than the black spots on an oak leaf. Yi was quite impressed by the delicacy of this craftsmanship.

"What is this?" Yi couldn't help but be curious and couldn't resist asking.

The one with the rectangular board pointed to the bamboo strip and recited fluently, "Naked debauchery, immoral disregard for rituals, bestial behavior. The country has constant punishment, only prohibition!"

Nüwa gave a sly glance at the small rectangular board and inwardly laughed at herself for asking something so absurd. Yi already knew that it was futile to engage in conversation with such things. So she remained silent and casually placed the bamboo strip on top of the board above its head. Then she reached into the forest of fire trees and pulled out a burning tree, intending to ignite the reed pile.

Suddenly, Yi heard a sobbing sound, a peculiar sound she had never heard before. She glanced down again and saw two tiny tears in the small eyes beneath the rectangular board. Because it was different from the crying sound she was accustomed to hearing, the "nga nga" cry, she didn't realize that this too was a form of crying.

Yi proceeded to light the fire, and not just in one place. The fire didn't blaze fiercely because the reeds were not completely dry, but it crackled and crackled for a long time. Eventually, countless tongues of flames emerged, stretching and licking upward, gradually forming a magnificent flower of flames and transforming into a pillar of fire. The towering flames overwhelmed the red glow on Kunlun Mountain. Suddenly, a strong wind arose, and the column of fire spun and roared. The green and multicolored stones turned uniformly red, spreading like molten caramel in the cracks, resembling an eternal lightning bolt.

The wind and the fire whipped Yi's hair, causing it to scatter and spin. Sweat poured down like a waterfall, and the intense flames illuminated her body, revealing the ultimate shade of flesh-red in the universe.

The column of fire gradually ascended, leaving only a heap of ash from the reed pile. Yi waited until the sky turned a clear blue before reaching out to touch it, but her fingertips still felt somewhat uneven.

"I've regained my strength, so I'll try again...," Yi thought to herself.

Yi bent down to gather the reed ash, filling it handful by handful into a large pool of water on the ground. The ash was still warm, steaming and bubbling in the water, splashing over Yi's entire body. The strong wind continued, carrying ash with it, turning Yi into the color of ash and soil.

"Phew!..." Yi let out her final breath.

In the blood-red clouds on the horizon, there was a radiant sun, a shimmering golden sphere encapsulated in ancient molten lava. On the other side, there was a cold, white moon resembling solid iron. But it was unknown who was descending and who was ascending. At this moment, Yi, having exhausted her entire being, lay down in between, no longer breathing.

In all directions, there was a silence surpassing death.

CHAPTER 3

One day, despite the bitterly cold weather, a commotion was heard. It was the imperial army finally arriving. Because they had waited for the absence of fire and smoke, they arrived late. They wielded yellow axes on the left and black axes on the right, with an enormous, ancient banner at the rear. They cautiously approached the lifeless body of Nüwa, but there was no movement to be seen. They set up camp on the belly of the corpse because it was the most fertile spot, showing their astuteness in selecting the location. However, they suddenly changed their tune, claiming that only they were the legitimate faction of Nüwa. They even altered the inscription on the banner to read "Intestines of Nüwa."

The old Taoist who had landed on the coast had passed on this tale through countless generations. Only on his deathbed did he impart the news to his disciples about the immortal mountain being carried by giant turtles to the sea. The disciples passed it on to their grandchildren, and later a sorcerer sought to gain favor by reporting it to Emperor Qin Shi Huang. Qin Shi Huang ordered the sorcerer to search for it.

The sorcerer could not find the immortal mountain, and Qin Shi Huang eventually died. Emperor Han Wu also ordered a search, but it yielded no results.

Apparently, the giant turtles did not understand Nüwa's words and merely nodded occasionally by chance. After stumbling through the journey in a daze, everyone scattered to sleep, and the immortal mountain sank along with them. Therefore, up until now, no one has ever seen even a fragment of the divine mountain, at most stumbling upon a few uncivilized islands.

November 1922.

SHATTERED DEPARTURE: A FRAGMENTED MEMOIR

If I could, I would write down my regrets and sorrows, for my dear child and for myself.

The dilapidated house, forgotten within the premises, is so silent and empty. Time passes by so quickly. I loved my dear child, relying on her to escape this silence and emptiness. It has already been a year. But how unfortunate it is that upon my return, this room is the only one left empty. The same broken window, the half-withered locust tree and the old purple wisteria outside the window, the square table in front of the window, the crumbling walls, and the board bed leaning against the wall—everything remains the same. Lying alone on the bed in the deep night, it feels as if the past year, spent with my dear child, never happened. I never moved out of this broken house and never established a hopeful little home in Jizhao Alley.

Not only that. A year ago, this silence and emptiness were not the same. They often carried anticipation, anticipating the arrival of my dear child. In the restless anticipation, the sound of high-heeled shoes tapping on the brick road would instantly invigorate me. I would then see her pale round face with a smiling trace, her thin pale arms, her striped blouse, and her dark skirt. She would bring the new leaves of the half-withered locust tree outside the window, allowing me to see them, as well as the purple and white wisteria flowers hanging on the iron-like old trunk.

But now, only the silence and emptiness remain. My dear child will never come back, never, forever!...

When my dear child is not in this broken house, I cannot see anything. In my boredom, I randomly grab a book, be it a scientific or literary one, it doesn't matter. I read on, read on, and suddenly I realize that I've flipped through more than ten pages, yet I don't remember anything the book says. However, my ears are exceptionally sensitive, as if I can hear the footsteps of everyone coming and going outside the front gate. From among them, I hear my dear child's footsteps, gradually approaching—clack, clack—but often fading away, eventually disappearing amidst the bustling footsteps of others. I detest the son of the neighbor who wears cloth-bottomed shoes and doesn't have footsteps resembling my dear child's. I detest the little one in the neighboring courtyard who often wears new leather shoes and applies snow-white cream, as his footsteps are too similar to my dear child's!

Could it be that she had a car accident? Could it be that she was hit by a tram?...

I wanted to grab my hat and go see her, but her cousin had previously insulted me to my face.

Suddenly, her footsteps approached, each step echoing one after another. When she came into view, she had already walked past the pergola of purple wisteria, her face adorned with a dimpled smile. It seemed she had not been mistreated at her uncle's house. My heart became calm, and after a silent exchange of glances, my voice filled the broken house. We talked about family tyranny, breaking old customs, gender equality, Ibsen, Tagore, Shelley... She always smiled and nodded, her eyes filled with innocent curiosity. On the wall hung a cut-out image of Shelley's bust, taken from a magazine, his most beautiful likeness. When I pointed it out to her, she only gave it a quick glance and lowered her head, seemingly embarrassed. In these matters, my dear child was perhaps still bound by old thoughts. Later, I thought it might be better to replace it with a memorial image of Shelley drowned at sea or one of Ibsen, but in the end, I never made the switch. Now, even that image is nowhere to be found.

"I am my own person, and no one has the right to interfere with my rights!"

This was after half a year of our acquaintance when we discussed her cousin here and her father at home. After a brief moment of contemplation, she spoke these words clearly, firmly, and calmly. By that time, I had expressed all my opinions, my background, my flaws, with little concealment, and she fully understood. Those few words shook my soul, resonating in my ears for many days, filling me with indescribable joy. I knew then that Chinese women were not as helpless as the pessimists claimed. In the near future, we would witness the dawn of brilliance.

As I walked her to the door, as usual, we maintained a distance of more than ten steps. As usual, that old man with catfish whiskers pressed his dirty face against the window glass, his nose flattened into a small plane. In the outer courtyard, as usual, there was that small face in the shiny glass window, adorned with thicker snow-white cream. She walked proudly, her eyes straight ahead, without glancing in his direction. I returned proudly.

"I am my own person, and no one has the right to interfere with my rights!" This thought resonated in her mind, clearer and stronger than in mine. What could half a bottle of snow-white cream and a small plane formed by a flattened nose mean to her?

I can no longer remember how I expressed my pure and passionate love to her at that time. Not only now, even back then it has become a blur, fragments that remain in fragments when I recall them at night. Within one or two months of living together, even these fragments turned into untraceable dreamlike images. I only remember the first ten or so days before that, when I carefully studied my attitude of expression, the order of my words, and the possible scenarios if met with rejection. But in the moment, it seemed all futile. In my nervousness, I involuntarily resorted to methods I had seen in movies. Later, I felt ashamed when I thought about it, but in my memory, only this one thing remains eternally present, like a solitary lamp in a dark room, illuminating me as I held her hand with tears in my eyes and knelt down on one leg…

It wasn't just my own words and actions, but also hers, that I couldn't clearly comprehend at that time. I only knew that she had allowed me. However, I still vaguely remember her complexion turning pale, then gradually becoming flushed—a flush I never saw again or since. Her childlike eyes emitted a mix of sadness and joy, tinged with a hint of doubt, though she tried to avoid my gaze, looking flustered as if wanting to fly through the window. Yet, I knew she had allowed me, but I didn't know how she said it or if she said it at all.

But she remembered everything — my words, to the point of being able to recite them fluently, as if they were deeply ingrained. She remembered my actions as if there were an unseen film playing before her eyes, narrated vividly, down to the minutest details, even including that fleeting moment from the shallow film that I never wanted to think about again. Late at night, when everything was quiet, it was time for her to review, and I would often be interrogated, tested, and commanded to repeat the words from that time, but she would often have to fill in the gaps, correct me, like an average student.

Over time, this reviewing became less frequent. But whenever I saw her gaze into the air, lost in deep thought, her expression softened and her dimples deepened, I knew she was revisiting old lessons on her own. However, I was afraid she might catch a glimpse of that ridiculous moment from the film. Yet, I also knew she had to see it, and it was unavoidable.

However, she didn't find it ridiculous. Even if I thought it was ridiculous, even despicable, she didn't find it ridiculous at all. I know this very well because she loved me with such fervor, such innocence.

The late spring of last year was the happiest and busiest time. My heart became calm, but another part of me became busy along with my body. It was during this time that we walked together on the streets, visited the park a few times, and mostly searched for a place to live. I felt that while walking on the streets, I encountered looks of curiosity, mockery, lewdness, and contempt. Unintentionally, my whole body would shrink a bit, and I had to immediately summon my pride and resistance to support myself. But she was fearless, completely indifferent to all of this, calmly proceeding as if entering an uninhabited realm.

Finding a place to live was not an easy task. Most of the time, we were met with excuses for rejection, and the rest we deemed unsuitable. At first, we made strict selections—which were not truly strict because they didn't seem like suitable places for us. Later on, we became more lenient, as long as they were tolerable. After looking at more than twenty places, we finally found a temporary dwelling in two southern rooms of a small house in Jizhao Hutong. The owner was a minor official, but he was a reasonable person who lived in the main house with his wife and a girl who was less than a year old. They employed a maid from the countryside, and as long as the child didn't cry, it was extremely peaceful and quiet.

Our furniture was very simple, but it had already consumed most of the funds I had raised. Zijun even sold her only gold ring and earrings. I tried to stop her, but she insisted on selling them. I no longer persisted because I knew that without contributing something of her own, she wouldn't feel comfortable living there.

With her uncle, she had already caused such a commotion that he was no longer willing to acknowledge her as his niece. I also gradually cut ties with several friends who considered themselves well-meaning advisers but were actually driven by their own timidity or even jealousy. However, it became peaceful as a result. After work each day, even though it was already close to dusk and the carriage driver always seemed to go so slowly, we still had moments alone together. We would first silently gaze into each other's eyes, then engage in intimate and heartfelt conversations, and eventually fall silent again. We would lower our heads, lost in thought, without really thinking about anything specific. Over the course of just three weeks, I seemed to have come to know her even better, gaining a deeper understanding of her body and her soul, shedding many of the previous misconceptions that I thought were understanding but now appeared to be barriers—true barriers.

Zijun also became more lively with each passing day. However, she didn't love flowers. The two potted plants I bought at the temple fair withered and died in a corner after four days of neglect, as I didn't have the leisure to tend to everything. However, she loved animals, perhaps influenced by the landlady. Within a month, our little household suddenly grew with the addition of four young chickens, mingling in the small courtyard with more than ten others belonging to the homeowner. Yet, she could recognize the appearance of each chicken and knew which one belonged to us. There was also a speckled dog that we bought at the fair. It seemed to have a previous name, but Zijun gave it a new one—Ah Sui. I also called it Ah Sui, although I didn't particularly like that name.

It is true, love must be constantly renewed, nurtured, and created. I discussed this with Zijun, and she nodded in understanding.

Ah, what a peaceful and blissful night it was!

Peace and happiness have the tendency to solidify, becoming everlasting in their tranquility and joy. When we were at the meeting hall, there were occasional conflicts and misunderstandings in our discussions, but since we moved to Jizhao Hutong, even that has disappeared. We only reminisce about those moments of conflict and the subsequent pleasure of reconciliation while sitting together under the lamp.

Zijun actually gained weight, and her complexion became rosy. Unfortunately, she was busy. Managing household chores left no time for leisurely conversations, let alone reading and strolling. We often said that we still needed to hire a maid.

This made me equally unhappy. When I came back in the evening, I often saw her hiding her unhappiness, especially when she tried to force a smile. Fortunately, I found out that it was still due to the hidden conflict with the small official's wife, triggered by the chickens from both households. But why did she have to keep it from me? Everyone should have an independent family. This kind of place is not suitable for living.

My routine was also set. Six days a week, I would go from home to the office and then back home. At the office, I would sit in front of my desk and handle paperwork and letters. At home, I would either sit across from her or help her with household chores, such as starting the stove, cooking meals, and steaming buns. I learned how to cook during this time.

But the quality of my food was much better than when I was at the meeting hall. Although cooking was not Zijun's forte, she put all her efforts into it. I couldn't help but share her concerns and consider it part of our shared joys and sorrows. Moreover, she would sweat profusely throughout the day, with short hair sticking to her forehead, and her hands becoming rough.

Furthermore, we had to take care of Ah Sui, take care of the chickens... all of these tasks were necessary and couldn't be done without her.

I had advised her before: if I don't eat, it's fine, but she must not work so hard. She glanced at me, remained silent, but her expression seemed somewhat sorrowful. I had no choice but to remain silent as well. However, she continued to toil like this.

The blow I had anticipated finally came. On the eve of Double Tenth Festival, I sat still while she washed the dishes. When I heard a knock on the door and went to open it, it was the office messenger who handed me a typewritten note. I had a hunch about its contents, and when I looked at it under the light, it confirmed my suspicions:

"By order of the Bureau Chief, Shi Juansheng is not required to report to the office.

Secretary's Office, October 9th."

I had already anticipated this back at the meeting hall. That snowflake paste was the gambling friend of the Bureau Chief's son, and he must have spread some rumors and tried to report on me. It was only now taking effect, which could be considered quite late. Actually, I didn't see it as a blow because I had already decided that I could write for others, teach, or even struggle to do translation work. Moreover, I had met the chief editor of "Friend of Liberty" a few times, and we had corresponded through letters two months ago. But my heart was pounding. Even that fearless Zijun had changed, which pained me greatly. She seemed more timid lately.

"What does that matter? Hmph, we'll do something new. We..." she said.

She didn't finish her sentence. Somehow, her voice sounded distant to me, and the light seemed particularly dim. Humans are truly funny creatures. Even the tiniest of things can have a profound impact on them. We stared at each other in silence and gradually began discussing. Eventually, we decided to save as much money as possible, both by placing "small advertisements" to seek writing and teaching opportunities and by writing a letter to the chief editor of "Friend of Liberty" to explain my current situation and request the publication of my translations, seeking his assistance during this difficult time.

"Let's do it! Let's open a new path!"

I immediately turned to the writing desk and pushed aside the bottle of fragrant oil and the vinegar dish. Zijun handed me the dim lamp. First, I drafted the advertisement; then I selected books that could be translated. Since the move, I hadn't had a chance to read any of them, and dust covered the top of each book. Finally, I wrote the letter.

I hesitated and struggled, unsure of how to word it. As I paused to contemplate, I glanced at her face. In the dim lamplight, her expression was filled with sorrow. I truly didn't expect such a small matter to bring about such a significant change in the resolute and fearless Zijun. She had truly become more timid lately, but it didn't start tonight. My heart became even more chaotic. Suddenly, images of a peaceful life flashed before my eyes — the silence of the dilapidated house in the meeting hall. I wanted to focus and examine it, but I saw only the dim light again.

After a long while, the letter was finally written, and it turned out to be quite lengthy. I felt tired, as if I had become more timid lately as well. So we decided to put the advertisement and the letter into action together the next day. Everyone straightened their backs simultaneously, silently sensing each other's resilience and strong spirits. We glimpsed the budding hope of the future.

The external blow actually revitalized our newfound spirit. Life in the office was like a bird held by a bird seller, barely surviving on a little bit of millet, never fattening up. Over time, its wings became numb, and even if released from the cage, it could no longer soar. Now we had finally escaped from this cage. From now on, I would soar in the new, vast sky, while I still remembered the beating of my wings.

The small advertisement wouldn't have an immediate effect, but translating books was not an easy task. What I had thought I understood from previous readings suddenly became perplexing and progress was slow. However, I was determined to work hard. In less than half a month, a large area of my fingertips turned dark, marking the tangible progress of my work. The chief editor of "Friend of Liberty" had once said that they would never bury good manuscripts.

Unfortunately, I don't have a quiet room, and Zijun is not as peaceful and considerate as before. The room is always cluttered with dishes and filled with coal smoke, making it difficult to focus on work. But naturally, I can only blame myself for not being able to afford a study room. However, there's also Ah Sui and the oil chickens to add to the chaos. The oil chickens have grown larger, becoming an even easier trigger for arguments between the two families.

In addition, there's the daily routine of endless meals. It seems that Zijun's accomplishments are completely based on these meals. We eat to raise money, and with the money, we eat. We also have to feed Ah Sui and the oil chickens. It's as if she has forgotten everything she knew before and doesn't consider that my thoughts are often interrupted by the urgency to eat. Even if I show a bit of anger, she doesn't change and continues to chew away as if completely unaffected.

It took five weeks to make her understand that my work cannot be bound by scheduled mealtimes. After she understood, she was probably unhappy, but she didn't say anything. My work indeed progressed more quickly from then on. In no time, I had translated fifty thousand words. After a round of polishing, I could send them along with the two completed essays to "Friend of Liberty." However, the issue of meals continued to trouble me. Cold dishes were tolerable, but sometimes there wasn't enough food, even though my appetite had significantly decreased since I spent the whole day at home using my brain. I had to feed Ah Sui first and sometimes even sheep meat that I could easily go without these days. She said Ah Sui had become too thin, and the landlady laughed at us because of it. She couldn't bear such ridicule.

So the only ones eating my leftovers were the oil chickens. It took me a while to realize this, but at the same time, I became aware of my position here, similar to Huxley's statement on "the position of humankind in the universe": I was nothing more than a watchdog between the oil chickens.

Later, after numerous struggles and pressures, the oil chickens gradually became our food. We and Ah Sui enjoyed more than ten days of fresh and fatty meals, but in reality, they were still quite lean because they could only get a few grains of sorghum each day. From then on, it became much quieter. Only Zijun seemed depressed, constantly feeling miserable and bored, to the extent that she was reluctant to speak. I thought, how easily people can change!

But Ah Sui couldn't stay either. We could no longer hope for letters from anywhere, and Zijun had long since run out of food to entice it to scratch or stand upright. Winter was approaching so quickly, and the stove was becoming a big problem. Its appetite had already become a heavy burden for us. So even it couldn't be kept anymore.

If we took it to the market and sold it as grass fodder, we might get a few coins, but neither of us could or wanted to do that. In the end, we covered it with a bundle and I took it to the western outskirts to release it, then came back and pushed it into a not-so-deep pit.

When I returned to the lodging, I felt much quieter, but Zijun's miserable expression surprised me. It was a look I had never seen before, undoubtedly because of Ah Sui. But why to this extent? I hadn't even mentioned putting it in the pit.

By nightfall, her miserable expression grew even colder.

"Strange. Zijun, why are you like this today?" I couldn't help but ask.

"What?" She didn't even look at me.

"Your complexion..."

"There's nothing... nothing at all."

Finally, from her words and actions, I realized that she probably thought I was a heartless person. In reality, I could live easily on my own. Although I was proud and never socialized with others, and even distanced myself from all the old acquaintances after moving, as long as I could spread my wings and fly high, there would still be plenty of opportunities. Now, enduring the pain of this oppressive life, most of it was for her. Even releasing Ah Sui was no different. But Zijun's understanding seemed to have become shallow, to the point where she couldn't even grasp this.

I seized an opportunity to imply these reasons to her, and she nodded as if understanding. However, based on her subsequent behavior, she either didn't understand or didn't believe it.

The cold weather and the coldness in her demeanor forced me to seek shelter outside the household. But where could I go? On the main road, in the park, although there was no coldness in the expression, the cold wind still cut through the skin. Finally, I found my paradise in the popular library.

There, there's no need to buy a ticket; the reading room is equipped with two iron stoves. Even though they only burn coal without much life, just seeing them there gives a sense of warmth. However, there are no good books to read: the old ones are stale, and there are hardly any new ones.

Fortunately, I didn't go there to read. There are often a few other people, sometimes more than ten, all wearing thin clothes like me. Each person reads their own book, using it as an excuse to keep warm. This arrangement suits me well. It's easy to encounter familiar faces on the streets, receiving disdainful glances, but there is no such misfortune here because they are forever huddled around other iron stoves or leaning against their own white stoves.

Although there are no books for me to read there, it still offers me a peaceful place to contemplate. When I sit alone and reminisce about the past, I realize that for the past half year, I have neglected all the essential aspects of life for the sake of love—blind love. The first of these aspects is living. One must live for love to have something to attach to. There are paths in the world opened for those who strive; I haven't forgotten the fluttering of wings, even though it has become much more feeble than before…

The room and the readers gradually disappear, and I see fishermen in raging waves, soldiers in trenches, the privileged on motorcycles, speculators in foreign lands, heroes in deep mountains and dense forests, professors on lecterns, athletes in the dark night, and thieves in the late hours... But Zijun is not nearby. She has lost all her courage, consumed by sorrow for Ah Sui and lost in her cooking. Strangely enough, she doesn't seem to have lost much weight...

As it grows colder, the few remaining pieces of unburned coal in the stove finally burn out; it's closing time. I have to return to Jizhao Alley and experience the cold colors once again. Occasionally, I encounter warm expressions, but it only increases my pain. I remember one night when a long-lost innocence flickered in Zijun's eyes, and she laughed as she spoke to me about our time at the association. Yet, she also had a hint of terror in her expression. I know that my recent coldness towards her has raised her suspicions, so I try my best to joke and bring her some comfort. However, as soon as my smile appears on my face and my words leave my mouth, they immediately turn hollow, echoing back at me with a bitter and mocking coldness.

Zijun seemed to feel it too, and from then on, she lost her usual numb calmness. Despite her efforts to conceal it, she often revealed an expression of worry and doubt, but she became much kinder towards me.

I wanted to tell her the truth, but I still didn't dare. Every time I mustered the courage to speak, I saw the childlike look in her eyes, which forced me to put on a forced expression of joy. But this immediately turned into a mocking coldness, causing me to lose my indifferent calmness.

She began revisiting the past and subjecting me to new tests, forcing me to give many insincere displays of affection, while the drafts of insincerity were written on my own heart. My heart gradually became filled with these drafts, making it difficult to breathe. In my distress, I often thought that speaking the truth naturally requires great courage. If one lacks this courage and settles for falsehood, they become someone incapable of forging a new path. Not only that, such a person never truly exists!

Zijun had a resentful expression, in the morning, on an extremely cold morning, something I had never seen before, but perhaps it was a resentful expression from my perspective. At that moment, I felt cold anger and sneered inwardly. Her cultivated thoughts and fearless and open-minded words were ultimately empty, and she was unaware of this emptiness. She no longer read any books, no longer knew that the first move in the game of life is to survive. Towards this path of survival, one must either join hands with others or go alone. If one only clings to the hem of another person's clothes, even a soldier will find it difficult to fight and can only perish together.

I felt that our new hope lay only in our separation; she should decisively let go—I suddenly thought of her death, but immediately reproached myself and repented. Luckily, it was morning, there was plenty of time, and I could speak my truth. The opening of our new path lies in this encounter.

We chatted casually, deliberately bringing up our past, mentioning literature, and then touching on foreign writers and their works: "Nora," "Madame Butterfly." We praised Nora's decisiveness... It was still the same conversation we had in the dilapidated house at the association last year, but now it had become empty. The words passed from my mouth to my own ears, and I suspected there was an invisible malicious child, whispering evil words behind my back.

She nodded in agreement and listened, then fell silent. I spoke intermittently, and even the echoes disappeared into the void.

"Yes," she remained silent for a moment and said, "but... Nian Sheng, I feel that you've changed a lot lately. Am I right? Can you honestly tell me?"

I felt as if I had been dealt a blow, but immediately regained my composure and expressed my opinions and beliefs: the opening of a new path, the reconstruction of a new life, in order to avoid perishing together.

In the end, with great determination, I added these words:

"...Moreover, you no longer need to worry and can move forward with courage. You asked me to be honest; yes, one should not be hypocritical. I will be honest: because, because I no longer love you! But it's much better for you, as you can carry on without any concerns..."

I anticipated a great upheaval, but there was only silence. Her face suddenly turned pale, as if lifeless. In an instant, she revived and her eyes gleamed with a childlike brightness. Her gaze darted around, seeking maternal affection like a hungry child, but only searching in emptiness and fearfully avoiding my eyes.

I couldn't bear to look any longer. Luckily, it was morning, and I braved the cold wind and headed straight to the public library.

There, I saw "Friend of Freedom," and my essays were published. It surprised me and gave me a glimmer of life. I thought, there are still many paths in life, but for now, it's not enough.

I began to visit old acquaintances whom I hadn't heard from in a long time, but it only happened once or twice. Their houses were naturally warm, but I felt a chilling coldness in my bones. At night, I curled up in a room colder than ice.

The icy needles pierced my soul, causing me perpetual pain and numbness. There are still many paths in life, and I haven't forgotten the flapping of wings, I think. Suddenly, I thought of her death, but immediately reproached myself and repented.

In the public library, I often caught glimpses of a fleeting light, a new path lying ahead. She awakened with courage, decisively stepping out of this cold home, and with a countenance devoid of resentment. I felt light as a passing cloud, floating in the sky, with the azure heavens above and deep mountains, vast seas, towering buildings, battlefields, motorcycles, foreign quarters, mansions, bustling markets, and dark nights below...

And truly, I had a premonition that this new face of life was about to arrive.

We finally survived the extremely unbearable winter, this Beijing winter. It was like a dragonfly falling into the mischievous hands of a naughty child, being toyed with and mistreated while tied with a thin thread. Although luckily it didn't lose its life, it still ended up lying on the ground, fighting for its survival.

I had written three letters to the chief editor of "Friend of Freedom," and finally received a reply, but the envelope contained only two book vouchers: a two-cent one and a three-cent one. Yet, even with my constant urging, it took nine cents in stamps, a day of hunger, and all ended up in vain, leaving me with nothing but emptiness.

However, the feeling that something was about to happen finally came true.

It was an event at the transition between winter and spring, when the wind was no longer as cold. I lingered outside for a longer time. By the time I returned home, it was probably already dusk. On one such gloomy evening, I came back as usual, feeling listless. As soon as I saw the door of my residence, my spirits sank even further, causing my footsteps to slow down. But eventually, I entered my own room, only to find it dark. When I struck a match, an unusual loneliness and emptiness filled the space.

In the midst of my bewilderment, Madame Guan came to the window and called me outside.

"Today, Subao's father came here and took her back," she said simply.

This seemed to be unexpected news, and I felt as if a blow had struck me from behind, standing there speechless.

"Did she leave?" I finally managed to ask after a while.

"She left."

"What did she say? Did she say anything?"

"She didn't say anything. She just asked me to tell you when you came back that she had gone."

I couldn't believe it, but there was an unusual loneliness and emptiness in the room. I searched everywhere for Subao; only a few worn-out and dim furniture pieces remained, appearing incredibly vacant, proving their inability to hide anyone or anything. I searched for any signs or writings left by her, but there were none.

Instead, salt and dried chili peppers, flour, half a cabbage, and a pile of copper coins were gathered in one place. These were the entirety of our living supplies, and now she solemnly left them for me alone, silently instructing me to use them to sustain my life for a while.

I felt as though I was being pushed away by my surroundings and rushed to the middle of the courtyard, where it was dark. The paper windows of the main house reflected bright light, as they were joking with children. My heart also grew calm, feeling a faint glimpse of escape from the heavy pressure: deep mountains and rivers, foreign quarters, feasts under electric lights, trenches, the darkest of nights, the strike of a blade, footsteps without a sound...

My mind became somewhat relaxed and at ease, thinking about the travel expenses and letting out a sigh of relief.

Lying down, the anticipated visions of the future passed by my closed eyes, and before midnight, they had already faded away. Suddenly, in the darkness, I seemed to see a pile of food, and afterwards, the pale face of Subao emerged, her childlike eyes wide open, looking at me pleadingly. I was in a trance, and everything disappeared.

But my heart felt heavy again. Why couldn't I endure a few more days and rush to tell her the truth like this? Now she knew, and all that awaited her in the future was the scorching sun-like severity of her father, the creditor of his own child, and the icy gazes of others. Besides that, there was emptiness. Bearing the burden of emptiness, walking the path of so-called life amidst severity and cold gazes, how terrifying it was! And to make matters worse, the end of this path was nothing but a grave without even a tombstone.

I shouldn't have revealed the truth to Subao. We had loved each other, and I should have devoted myself to lying to her forever. If truth could be cherished, it wouldn't have been such a heavy emptiness for Subao. Lies, of course, were also emptiness, but at most, they would have been this heavy in the end.

I thought that by telling the truth to Subao, she could fearlessly and resolutely move forward without any worries, just as we had planned when we were going to live together. But I was probably mistaken. Her bravery and fearlessness at that time were because of love.

I didn't have the courage to bear the burden of hypocrisy, but I unloaded the burden of truth onto her. After she loved me, she had to bear this burden and walk the path of so-called life amidst severity and cold gazes.

I thought of her death... I saw that I was a coward, deserving to be rejected by powerful people, whether they were truthful or deceitful. Yet, she had always hoped that I would sustain my life for a while...

I want to leave Jizhao Hutong; there is an unusual emptiness and loneliness here. I think that as long as I leave this place, Subao will still be by my side; at least, she will still be in the city and one day unexpectedly visit me, just like when she lived in the association hall.

However, all my requests and letters received no response. I had no choice but to visit an old friend who I hadn't seen in a long time. He was a childhood classmate of my uncle, known for being serious and well-respected, having lived in Beijing for a long time and having a wide social circle.

Perhaps because of my shabby clothes, the gatekeeper gave me a disdainful look when I arrived. It was difficult to finally meet him, and even then, it was distant. He knew all about our past.

"Of course, you can't stay here," he said coldly after hearing my request for help in finding a job elsewhere. "But where can you go? It's not easy... And your friend, Subao, do you know? She's dead."

I was speechless with shock.

"Really?" I finally asked involuntarily.

"Haha. Naturally, it's true. My Wang Sheng's family is from the same village as hers."

"But... do you know how she died?"

"Who knows? All I know is that she's dead."

I have forgotten how I said goodbye to him and returned to my dwelling. I knew he wasn't lying; Subao would never come back, like she did last year. Although she wanted to bear the burden of emptiness amidst severity and cold gazes and walk the path of so-called life, she couldn't anymore. Her fate had already decided that she would perish in the truth I gave her—a loveless world!

Naturally, I couldn't stay here, but "where can I go?"

Surrounded by vast emptiness and the silence of death, I seem to see it all, the darkness before the eyes of those who die without love. I hear the struggles of all the anguish and despair.

I still anticipate the arrival of something new, unnamed and unexpected. But day after day, it is nothing but the silence of death.

I rarely go out anymore, just sitting and lying down in this vast emptiness, allowing the silence of death to erode my soul. Sometimes, even the silence of death trembles and hides itself, and in those rare moments, in this interlude of desolation, unnamed, unexpected, new hopes flash before me.

One day, it was a gloomy morning, the sun struggling to break through the clouds, even the air felt weary. I heard faint footsteps and wheezing breaths, which made me open my eyes. Upon a quick glance, the room was still empty, but then I noticed something on the floor—a small creature, thin and half-dead, covered in dust...

As I looked closely, my heart skipped a beat and then began to race.

It was Asui. It had returned.

Leaving Jizhao Hutong was not only because of the disdainful gazes of the landlords and their female workers but also largely because of Asui. But "where can I go?" There are still many new paths ahead, and I have a vague idea and occasionally glimpse them, feeling that they are right in front of me. However, I have yet to discover the method to take the first step into those paths.

After much contemplation and comparison, the association hall remains the only place where I can find solace. The same dilapidated house, the same wooden bed, the same half-withered locust tree and purple wisteria, but all the hope, joy, love, and vitality that used to fill me have vanished. Only emptiness remains, the emptiness I acquired in exchange for the truth.

There are still many new paths, and I must step into them because I am still alive. But I do not yet know how to take that first step. Sometimes, it seems as if the path of life is like a grayish-white serpent, winding its way towards me, and I wait, waiting to see it approach, but suddenly it disappears into the darkness.

The nights of early spring are still so long. In the long hours of sitting, I recall the funeral I witnessed in the morning on the street, with paper figures and horses at the front and cries that sounded like singing at the back. Now I understand their cleverness; it is such an effortless and straightforward matter.

However, Zijun's funeral appears once again before my eyes. I alone carry the burden of emptiness, walking on the gray-white long road, only to immediately disappear amidst the stern gazes and cold eyes around me.

I wish there were such things as ghosts and hell, so that even amidst the raging storms of karma, I could seek out Zijun and express my regret and sorrow to her face, begging for her forgiveness. Otherwise, the poisonous flames of hell will engulf me and mercilessly consume my regret and sorrow.

I will embrace Zijun in the midst of the storms and flames, pleading for her mercy, or perhaps granting her satisfaction...

But this is even more futile than the new paths. Right now, all there is, is the long night of early spring. I am alive, and I must take that first step towards the new paths. And that first step — will merely be to write down my regret and sorrow, for Zijun, for myself.

I still only have cries that sound like singing, accompanying Zijun's burial, buried in oblivion.

I want to forget; I do it for myself, and I no longer want to think about burying Zijun with forgetfulness.

I must take the first step towards the new paths, deeply burying the truth within the wounds of my heart, silently moving forward, guided by forgetfulness and lies...

October 21, 1925.

TO THE MOON

CHAPTER 1

The clever animal indeed understands human intentions. As soon as it sees the entrance gate, the horse immediately slows down its pace and lowers its head, step by step, as if pounding rice.

Dusk envelops the grand mansion, and thick black smoke rises from the neighboring houses; it's already dinner time. The house servants have heard the sound of hooves and have already come out, standing outside the gate with their hands hanging straight. Yi lazily dismounts near the garbage pile, and the servants take over the reins and whip. Just as he is about to step through the main gate, he looks down at the brand new pot hanging from his waist, filled with arrows, and the three black crows and a shattered sparrow in his net. He feels very hesitant. Nevertheless, he musters up his courage and walks in with big strides; the arrows jingle inside the pot.

As soon as he enters the inner courtyard, he sees Chang'e poking her head out of the round window. He knows her eyes are sharp, and she must have noticed the crows a long time ago. Startled, he stops in his tracks, but he has no choice but to continue walking. The maidservants come out to greet him, taking off his bow and arrows, and removing the net bag. He feels as though they are all smiling bitterly.

"Wife..." he wipes his face and walks into the inner chamber, calling out at the same time.

Chang'e is gazing at the twilight sky outside the round window. Slowly turning her head, she glances at him indifferently, without responding.

Yi is already accustomed to this kind of situation, at least for over a year now. He still approaches her and sits on the wooden couch opposite, covered with a furless leopard skin. He scratches his scalp and stammers, saying, "Today's luck is still not good, only crows..."

"Hmph!" Chang'e raises her eyebrows, suddenly stands up, and walks out like the wind, muttering, "Crows again for the black bean sauce noodles! Crows again for the black bean sauce noodles! Go and ask, whose family eats crow meat for black bean sauce noodles all year round? I really don't know what kind of luck I've had to end up marrying here and eating crow meat for black bean sauce noodles all year round!"

"Wife," Yi quickly stands up too, following behind and whispering, "But today was not bad. I also shot a sparrow, which can be used for cooking. Nuxin!" He loudly calls for the maid, "Bring that sparrow here for the wife to see!"

The game has already been taken to the kitchen, so Nuxin goes to fetch it, holding it in both hands and presenting it to Chang'e.

"Hmph!" She glanced at it, slowly squeezed it in her hand, and said unhappily, "It's a mess! Isn't it all shattered? Where's the meat?"

"Yes," Yi said fearfully, "It's shattered. My bow is too strong, and the arrowhead is too big."

"Can't you use smaller arrowheads?"

"I don't have smaller ones. Ever since I shot down the boar and the long snake..."

"Is this the long snake?" She said, turning her head to Nuxin and said, "Bring a bowl of soup!" Then she went back into the room.

Only Yi stayed dumbfounded in the hall, sitting against the wall, listening to the sound of exploding firewood in the kitchen. He remembered how big the boar was back then, like a small mound when seen from afar. If he hadn't shot and killed it, leaving it until now, it could have been eaten for half a year, and there would be no need to worry about food every day. And the long snake, it could have been made into a soup to drink...

Nu Yi came and lit the lamp. The vermilion bow, vermilion arrows, green bow, green arrows, crossbow, long sword, short sword, all appeared in the dim light on the opposite wall. Yi took a glance and lowered his head, sighing. He saw Nuxin bring in the dinner and placed it on the central table. On the left were five large bowls of plain noodles; on the right were two large bowls, one of soup; and in the middle was a large bowl of black bean sauce made from crow meat.

Yi ate the black bean sauce noodles, and he himself felt that they weren't delicious. He stole a glance at Chang'e, she didn't even look at the black bean sauce, she just soaked the noodles in the soup, ate half a bowl, and then set it down. He felt as if her face was paler and thinner than usual, fearing that she might be sick.

By the second watch of the night, she seemed to be a bit more amiable, sitting silently on the edge of the bed drinking water. Yi sat on the nearby wooden couch, rubbing the furless leopard skin with his hand.

"Alas," he said kindly, "This Western Mountain's leopards were all shot before we got married. They were so beautiful back then, shining with golden light." He then reminisced about the food from that time. They only ate four bear paws, kept the hump of a camel, and gave the rest to the maidservants and the house servants. After the big animals were shot, they ate wild boars, rabbits, and mountain chickens. His archery skills were exceptional, so he could shoot as much as he wanted. "Alas," he couldn't help but sigh, "My archery skills are truly marvelous. I shot everything till there was nothing left. Who would have expected that only crows would be left for cooking..."

"Hmph," Chang'e smiled faintly.

"Today, luck still has to be taken into account," Yi also became happy. "I actually managed to hunt down a sparrow. It took me a detour of thirty miles to find it."

"Can't you go even farther?"

"Yes, madam. I was thinking the same thing. Tomorrow, I plan to wake up earlier. If you wake up early, wake me up too. I'm prepared to go fifty miles away and see if there are any deer or rabbits... but it might be difficult. When I shot down the boar and the long snake, there were so many wild animals. You should still remember, in front of your mother's house, there were often black bears passing by, and I had to shoot them several times..."

"Is that so?" Chang'e seemed to not remember much.

"Who would have expected that they would be completely gone now. Thinking about it, I really don't know how we'll live in the future. For me, it doesn't matter as long as I take the golden elixir given to me by the Taoist and ascend. But first, I have to plan for you... so I've decided to go even farther tomorrow..."

"Hmph." Chang'e had finished drinking water, slowly lay down, and closed her eyes.

The dim light illuminated the remaining makeup, the powder had faded a bit, the eye circles appeared slightly yellow, and the color of the eyebrows seemed different on both sides. But her lips were still as red as fire; although she wasn't smiling, there were still shallow dimples on her cheeks.

"Ah, ah, such a person, I only give her black bean sauce noodles to eat all year round..." Yi thought and felt ashamed, his cheeks and ears turned hot.

CHAPTER 2

The next day arrived after a night's passing.

Yi suddenly opened his eyes and saw a beam of sunlight slanting on the west wall, knowing that it wasn't early anymore. He looked at Chang'e, who was still sprawled out sleeping. He quietly put on his clothes, got off the leopard skin couch, stepped out of the front hall, washing his face while instructing Nvgeng to tell Wang Sheng to prepare the horse.

Because he was busy with matters, he had long abandoned breakfast. Nv Yi put five pancakes, five onions, and a packet of spicy sauce in a net bag, along with his bow and arrows, all tied around his waist. He tightened his belt and lightly stepped out of the hall, telling Nv Geng, who was coming in from the opposite side:

"I plan to go to a distant place to search for food today. I may come back later. When the madam wakes up and has her morning snack and feels somewhat happy, you can go and inform her, saying that dinner will be delayed, and apologize profusely. Remember? You say: apologize profusely."

He quickly walked out, mounted his horse, leaving the guards behind without a second thought, and soon rode out of the village. Ahead was the sorghum field he was familiar with, but he paid no attention, knowing there was nothing there. With a flick of the reins, he galloped forward, covering about sixty miles. He saw ahead a cluster of lush trees, and his horse, panting and covered in sweat, naturally slowed down. After traveling for another ten miles or so, he finally approached the woods, but all he saw were wasps, butterflies, ants, and grasshoppers—no trace of any animals. When he saw this new area, he thought there would at least be one or two foxes or rabbits, but now he realized it was just wishful thinking. He had to circle around the woods and found that behind it was again a stretch of green sorghum fields, with a few small mud huts scattered in the distance. The wind was warm, the sun shining, and there was no sound of birds or sparrows.

"What bad luck!" he shouted as he let out his frustration.

But after taking a few more steps forward, his spirits immediately lifted. In the open space outside a mud hut, he saw a flying creature, pecking step by step, resembling a large pigeon. He hastily picked up his bow, loaded an arrow, pulled the string to full tension, and released it. The arrow shot out like a shooting star.

This was no time for hesitation; it always hit the mark. As long as he followed the path of the arrow on horseback, he would be able to retrieve his prey. However, to his surprise, as he approached, an old woman was already holding the arrow-struck big pigeon and shouting loudly as she rushed toward him, directly facing his horse's head.

"Who are you? How did you shoot my prized black hen? Why are your hands so idle?..."

Yi's heart skipped a beat, and he quickly pulled the reins.

"Oh, no! It was a chicken? I thought it was a quail," he said anxiously.

"You're blind! Look at you, you're over forty years old, right?"

"Yes, Madam. I turned forty-five last year."

"You're truly useless! You can't even recognize a hen and mistake it for a quail! Who exactly are you?"

"I am Yi Yi," he said, looking at the arrow he shot, which pierced the hen's heart, causing its death. The last two words were not said loudly. He dismounted from his horse.

"Yi Yi? Who's that? I don't know you," she said, looking at his face.

"Some people recognize me right away. During Emperor Yao's time, I shot and killed several wild boars and snakes..."

"Haha, liar! Those were killed by Fengmeng and others in partnership. Maybe you were involved too, but now you claim it was your own achievement. How shameless!"

"Oh, Madam. Fengmeng has been visiting me frequently in recent years, but we have no partnership or connection whatsoever."

"You're lying. People have been saying that I've heard about it four or five times in a month."

"Well, let's talk about serious matters. What should we do with this chicken?"

"Compensation. This is the best hen in my household, laying eggs every day. You must compensate me with two hoes and three spinning wheels."

"Madam, look at me. I don't farm or weave. Where would I get hoes and spinning wheels? I don't have money on me, only five pancakes made from white flour. I can give you those to compensate for your chicken, and I'll add five onions and a packet of sweet and spicy sauce. What do you think?" He reached into his net bag with one hand to take out the pancakes and extended his other hand to take the chicken.

The old woman saw the white flour pancakes and became somewhat willing, but she insisted on fifteen of them. After much negotiation, they finally agreed on ten, and it was decided that he would deliver them no later than noon tomorrow, using the arrow that shot the chicken as collateral. Yi finally felt relieved at this point. He stuffed the dead chicken into his net bag, mounted his saddle, and rode away. Although he was hungry, he felt quite pleased. They hadn't had chicken soup for over a year.

When he emerged from the woods, it was still afternoon. He urged his horse forward, but the horse was exhausted. Just as he approached the familiar sorghum field, it was already dusk. He saw a figure flash in the distance, followed by an arrow suddenly flying towards him.

Yi didn't rein in his horse, letting it run freely. At the same time, he drew his bow and aimed the arrow. With a single release, a metallic clang was heard as the arrowheads met in mid-air, producing a few sparks. The two arrows formed the shape of the Chinese character "人" (ren), then flipped and fell to the ground. Immediately after the first arrow touched, a second arrow came from both sides, once again clanging in mid-air. Nine arrows were shot in this manner until Yi ran out of arrows. However, by that time, he had already seen Fengmeng smugly standing on the opposite side, with one arrow still on his bowstring, aiming at Yi's throat.

"Haha, I thought he had gone to the seaside to fish. It turns out he's still engaged in these activities here. No wonder the old woman had those words..." Yi thought.

In an instant, the bow on the other side was like a full moon, and the arrow like a shooting star. With a swoosh, it flew towards Yi's throat. Perhaps the aim was slightly off, but it struck him right in the mouth. Yi somersaulted, falling from the horse, which then came to a stop.

Seeing that Yi was dead, Fengmeng slowly approached, smiling as he looked at Yi's lifeless face, savoring his victory like a glass of celebratory liquor.

Just as he was about to examine more closely, he saw Yi open his eyes and suddenly sit up.

"You've come for nothing a hundred times," he spat out the

arrow and laughed. "Don't tell me you're not familiar with my 'Gnawing Arrow' technique? This won't do. These little tricks won't work against me. You can't steal someone else's fist and expect to defeat the person. You need to practice on your own."

"To use their own methods against them..." the victor murmured softly.

"Hahaha!" Yi laughed heartily while standing up. "Quoting classic phrases again. But those words might fool the old woman, what good are they in front of me? I've always been a hunter, never engaging in your sneaky techniques...," he said, glancing at the hen in his net bag, which had not been crushed. He mounted his horse and rode away without hesitation.

"...You've struck a funeral bell!" came the distant curses and insults.

"I never expected such lack of character. At such a young age, he's already learned how to curse. No wonder the old woman trusted him so much," Yi thought, shaking his head in despair while riding his horse.

CHAPTER 3

Before Yi finished crossing the sorghum field, the sky had already darkened. Blue stars appeared in the sky, and Chang'e shone particularly bright in the western horizon. The horse could only follow the white field ridges, and it was already exhausted, naturally slowing down. Fortunately, the moon was gradually releasing its silver-white glow on the horizon.

"Annoying!" Yi heard his stomach rumble and became restless on the horse. "Just when I'm busy making a living, I always encounter these boring things, wasting my effort!" He nudged his legs against the horse's belly, urging it to go faster, but the horse only twisted its hindquarters and continued to move slowly.

"Chang'e must be angry. Look how late it is today," he thought.

"She might want to show me a certain expression. But luckily, I have this little hen to please her. I just need to say, 'Madam, I ran two hundred miles back and forth to find this.' No, that doesn't sound right. It seems too boastful."

He saw the lights of a house ahead and felt happy, so he stopped thinking further. The horse didn't need any urging and naturally galloped. The round, snowy-white moon illuminated the path, and the cool wind blew against his face, making it even more enjoyable than returning from a great hunt.

The horse naturally stopped by the garbage dump. Yi looked and felt something was strange, as if the house was in disarray. Only Zhao Fu came out to greet him.

"What's wrong? Where's Wang Sheng?" he asked curiously.

"Wang Sheng went to Yao's house to find Madam," Zhao Fu replied.

"What? Madam went to Yao's house?" Yi remained seated on the horse, asking in surprise.

"Uh...," Zhao Fu hesitated while answering, going to take the horse reins and whip.

Only then did Yi dismount and enter the house. He thought for a moment, then turned back to ask, "Didn't he wait impatiently and go to the restaurant himself?"

"Uh, I checked three restaurants. None of them saw him," Zhao Fu replied.

Yi lowered his head, pondered, and walked inside. The three maids were gathered in front of the hall, looking bewildered. He was very surprised and asked loudly, "Are all of you at home? Isn't it unusual for Madam to go to Yao's house alone?"

They didn't answer, just looked at his face, and proceeded to take off his quiver, flask, and the net bag containing the little hen. Yi suddenly felt his heart pounding, thinking that Chang'e might have done something rash out of anger. He asked Nü Geng to call Zhao Fu and have him check the tree in the pond in the backyard. But as soon as he stepped into the room, he knew that his speculation was incorrect. The room was also in disarray, the wardrobe was open, and a quick glance at the bed revealed the missing jewelry box. At that moment, it felt like a bucket of cold water was poured over his head. The gold and pearls were insignificant, but the elixir given to him by the Taoist was also kept in that jewelry box.

Yi paced in circles twice before seeing Wang Sheng standing outside the door.

"Sir," Wang Sheng said, "Madam did not go to Yao's house; they are not playing cards today either."

Yi glanced at him but remained silent. Wang Sheng then retreated.

"What did the master say?" Zhao Fu came up and asked.

Yi shook his head and waved his hand, signaling him to leave as well.

Yi paced in the room a few more times, walked to the front hall, sat down, and looked up at the crimson bow, crimson arrows, the green bow, the green arrows, crossbows, long swords, short swords on the opposite wall. After pondering for a while, he finally asked the maids standing below:

"When did Madam disappear?"

"She disappeared when the lamps were lit," Nü Yi said, "But no one saw her leave."

"Did any of you see her consume the medicine from that box?"

"We didn't see that. But in the afternoon, she asked me to pour her some water to drink," Nü Yi replied.

Yi stood up anxiously. It seemed as if he was left alone on the ground.

"Did any of you see anything ascending to the sky?" he asked.

"Oh!" Nü Xin thought for a moment and suddenly realized, "When I went out after lighting the lamps, I did see a dark shadow flying in this direction. But I never imagined it could be Madam..." Her face turned pale.

"That must be it!" Yi slapped his knee and immediately stood up, walked outside, and turned back to ask Nü Xin, "Which direction?"

Nü Xin pointed with her hand, and as he followed her gaze, he saw a round, snowy-white moon hanging in the sky. Faintly visible within it were pavilions and trees, reminiscent of the beautiful scenery in the Moon Palace that his grandmother used to tell him about when he was a child. Facing the moon floating in the azure sea, he felt an immense heaviness in his body.

He suddenly became angry. From that anger, a murderous intent arose. With his eyes wide open, he shouted loudly at the maidservants:

"Bring me my Sun-shooting Bow! And three arrows!"

Nü Yi and Nü Geng retrieved the powerful bow from the center of the hall, dusted it off, and handed him three long arrows.

He held the bow in one hand and grasped the three arrows in the other. He placed the arrows on the bowstring, pulled it back to full draw, directly aiming at the moon. His body stood upright like a rock, his gaze piercing, shining like lightning beneath the rocks. His hair fluttered in the wind, resembling black flames. In that instant, one could almost envision his heroic figure from the past when he shot down the sun.

With a swift "swoosh," in just one sound, he had already released three arrows. As soon as one arrow was released, another one was set, and as soon as it was set, another arrow was released. The eyes couldn't keep up with the speed, nor could the ears distinguish the sounds. Although the arrows had struck the moon, which should have gathered in one place due to the interlocking arrows, they split into three points, causing three wounds.

The maidservants let out a cry, and everyone saw the moon tremble, as if it were about to fall. But it remained hanging safely, emitting a brighter and more pleasant radiance, seemingly undamaged.

"Tsk!" Yi shouted at the sky, observing for a moment. However, the moon paid no attention to him. He took three steps forward, and the moon retreated three steps. He took three steps back, and the moon advanced by the same number.

They all fell silent, each person looking at the other's face.

Yi lazily leaned his Sun-shooting Bow against the hall door and walked back into the room. The maidservants followed suit.

"Alas," Yi sighed as he sat down, "So, your mistress will forever be alone and happy. She could bear to leave me behind and ascend alone? Could it be that she saw me growing old? But just last month, she said, 'You're not old yet. If you consider yourself old, it's the degradation of your thoughts.'"

"That can't be true," Nü Yi said, "Some say that the master is still a warrior."

"At times, he seems almost like an artist," Nü Xin added.

"Nonsense! But that crow's shredded pork noodles really aren't tasty. No wonder she couldn't resist..."

"I'll go cut a piece of leopard-skin rug by the wall to patch it up. It looks unsightly," Nü Xin said as she walked towards the room.

"Wait a moment," Yi said, after thinking for a while. "There's no rush. I'm extremely hungry, so let's quickly make a plate of spicy chicken and bake five pounds of pancakes for me to eat before going to sleep. Tomorrow, I'll go find that Taoist priest and ask for a dose of the elixir. After taking it, I'll catch up with her. Nü Geng, go instruct Wang Sheng to measure four liters of white beans to feed the horses!"

December 1926.

WHITE LIGHT

When Chen Shicheng looked at the list of county examinations, it was already afternoon by the time he returned home. He had gone early, and as soon as he saw the list, he searched for the characters "Chen Shicheng" on it. There were many instances of the name Chen, and they all seemed to jump into his eyes one after another, but none of them were the characters he was looking for. So he carefully searched again within the circular patterns on the twelve sheets of the list, but by the time he finished, everyone else had left, and Chen Shicheng still hadn't found his name. He stood alone in front of the wall of the examination hall.

Although a cool breeze gently brushed his gray hair, the early winter sun was still warm as it shone on him. However, he seemed to be dizzy from the sun, and his face grew increasingly pale. From his tired, swollen eyes, there emitted a strange gleam. At this moment, he wasn't actually seeing the text on the wall anymore; he only saw many dark circles floating and wandering before his eyes.

Talented scholars excelled in the provincial examination, went straight to the capital for the metropolitan examination, and quickly ascended through the ranks... Gentlemen from respectable families desperately sought to establish connections, and people now revered them as if they were deities, deeply regretting their previous indifference and confusion... They drove away the miscellaneous people who had been living in their dilapidated homes — not that anyone needed to chase them away; they left on their own accord — and now their houses were completely renovated, with flagpoles and inscribed plaques at the entrance... If one sought lofty positions, they could become officials in the capital; otherwise, it was better to seek opportunities elsewhere... The promising future that he had carefully planned suddenly collapsed like a water-soaked sugar tower, leaving only a pile of fragments. Unconsciously, he felt his disoriented body spinning, and he walked aimlessly towards his home.

Just as he reached his own doorstep, seven students

simultaneously began reciting their lessons at the top of their lungs. He was taken aback, feeling as if a bell had just tolled in his ear. He saw seven heads with braided hair swinging in front of his eyes, swinging throughout the entire room, with black circles dancing along. He sat down, and they came to present their evening lessons, each of their faces showing a hint of disdain towards him.

"Go back home," he hesitated for a moment before saying mournfully.

They hurriedly packed their schoolbags and ran away with them.

Chen Shicheng still saw many small heads with black circles dancing in front of his eyes, sometimes in chaos, sometimes forming peculiar formations, but gradually they decreased and blurred.

"It's over again!"

He was taken aback, jumping up in surprise. The words that were clearly near his ear, when he turned around, there was no one there, as if he had heard the tolling of a bell again, and his own mouth said:

"It's over again!"

Suddenly, he raised a hand and began counting on his fingers, eleven, thirteen times, even this year was the sixteenth time, yet not a single examiner understood his writing. They were blind, and it was a pitiful situation. He couldn't help but burst into laughter. However, he became furious and suddenly pulled out the meticulously copied "Zhizhi" and test papers from the bottom of his schoolbag, holding them as he walked out. Just as he approached the door, he saw everything around him bright and even a group of chickens laughing at him. His heart couldn't help but race frantically, so he had to retreat back inside.

He sat down again, his gaze flickering. He witnessed many things, but they were blurred. The collapsed sugar tower-like future lay before him, and this future only grew vast, blocking all his paths.

The smoke from other households' cooking had long dissipated, and the bowls and chopsticks had been washed, but Chen Shicheng still didn't go to cook. The people living here knew the old routine. Whenever the county examination came around, upon seeing the looks in people's eyes after the list was posted, it was better to close the door early and not meddle in affairs. First, all voices disappeared, followed by the gradual extinguishing of lights, leaving only the moon slowly appearing in the cold night sky.

The sky was as blue as a vast sea, with a few scattered clouds, swaying as if someone was washing chalk in a water container. The moon cast a cold wave of light upon Chen Shicheng. It was just like a newly polished iron mirror at first, but this mirror mysteriously reflected his entire body, projecting the shadow of an iron moon onto him.

He was still wandering in the courtyard outside the house, his eyes becoming somewhat clear, and the surroundings were quiet. But this silence suddenly became disturbed for no reason, and he distinctly heard a hurried and low voice saying:

"Turn left, turn right..."

He shuddered, and as he leaned in to listen, the voice repeated, this time slightly louder:

"Turn right!"

He remembered. This courtyard, before his home had fallen into such disrepair, during the summer nights, he and his grandmother would sit here in the courtyard to enjoy the coolness. At that time, he was just a ten-year-old child lying on a bamboo couch, while his grandmother sat beside him, telling him interesting stories. She would say that according to what she had heard from her own grandmother, the ancestors of the Chen family were wealthy, and this house was the foundation. The ancestors had buried countless silver coins, and it would be inherited by fortunate descendants. However, it had not been discovered to this day. As for the location, it was hidden within a riddle:

"Turn left, turn right, go forward, go backward, measure gold, measure silver, it doesn't matter who competes."

Regarding this riddle, Chen Shicheng had often speculated about it secretly in his spare time. Unfortunately, every time he thought he had found the answer, he immediately felt that it didn't fit. There was one time when he was certain it was hidden beneath the floor of the house rented to the Tang family, but he never had the courage to excavate it. After a while, he felt that it seemed too unlikely. As for the few old traces he had dug up in his own house, they were all impulsive actions that he had taken after several failed examinations. When he saw them later, he felt ashamed and embarrassed.

But today, the iron light enveloped Chen Shicheng and softly urged him. Perhaps hesitating for a moment, it would provide him with convincing proof and add a sinister sense of urgency, forcing him to turn his gaze back to his own room.

A white light, like a white folding fan, flickered and appeared in his room.

"Finally, it's here!"

He exclaimed and quickly rushed into the room like a lion. However, when he stepped inside, there was no trace of the white light. There was only a dim, old room with a few broken desks. He stood there, feeling refreshed, and slowly focused his gaze. Yet, the white light clearly reappeared, even more expansive this time, whiter and purer than sulfur fire, more ethereal than morning mist, and it was right under the desk against the east wall.

Chen Shicheng rushed to the back of the door, reaching out to grab the hoe and bumped into a black shadow. He felt a bit scared for some reason and anxiously turned on the light, only to find the hoe leaning against the wall. He moved the table aside and used the hoe to quickly dig up four large bricks. He squatted down and, as usual, there was fine yellow sand beneath, so he rolled up his sleeves and cleared away the sand, revealing the black soil underneath. He proceeded with extreme caution, in silence, digging one shovel at a time. However, the deep silence of the late night made the sound of the pointed iron hitting the soil unavoidably dull and heavy, refusing to be concealed.

The pit was now over two feet deep, but there was no sign of a jar mouth. Chen Shicheng became anxious, and with a loud noise that shook his wrist and caused pain, the hoe hit something hard. He quickly threw down the hoe and felt around, only to find a large brick underneath. His heart trembled intensely, and he focused his attention on digging up that brick. Below it was the same black soil, and after clearing away a lot of soil, it seemed to have no end. But suddenly, he touched something small and hard, round in shape, perhaps a rusty copper coin. There were also a few broken pieces of porcelain.

Chen Shicheng felt a sense of emptiness in his heart, his body covered in sweat, and he impatiently scratched himself. In the midst of this, his heart trembled in the air as he touched another strange little object, roughly shaped like a horse's hoof, but with a fragile touch. He carefully dug up that object and held it in his hand, carefully examining it under the light. The object was mottled, resembling rotten bones, with a row of scattered and incomplete teeth on it. He realized that it was a jawbone, and that jawbone moved and laughed in his hand, finally hearing it speak:

"This is it again!"

He shivered, feeling a sudden chill, and let go of the jawbone. It floated lightly back to the bottom of the pit, and he quickly escaped to the courtyard. He stole a glance at the house, where the lights were shining brightly and the jawbone was mocking him, an unusually frightening sight. He dared not look in that direction anymore. He hid in the shadow of a distant eave, feeling relatively safe. But in this sense of safety, he suddenly heard a whispered voice by his ear:

"It's not here... Go to the mountains..."

Chen Shicheng seemed to recall hearing someone say such words on the street during the day. Without waiting to hear the rest, he suddenly looked up at the sky. The moon had already disappeared towards the western peak. Far in the distance, about thirty-five miles away from the city, the western peak stood tall, pitch-black, emitting a vast shimmering white light.

And that white light was just ahead, in the distance.

"Yes, go to the mountains!"

He made up his mind and dashed out. After a few opening and closing door sounds, there was no longer any sound coming from inside the house. The lamp illuminated the empty room and the pit, sputtering a few times before gradually shrinking until it vanished completely, the residual oil having burned out.

"Open the city gates ~ ~ "

With a terrifying and desperate cry filled with hope, like a strand of silk in the dawn at the western gate, trembling and calling out.

The next day at noon, someone saw a floating corpse in Wanliu Lake, fifteen miles from the west gate. The news spread immediately and eventually reached the ears of the local authorities, who instructed the villagers to retrieve the body. It was the body of a man in his fifties, "beardless with a pale face," and he had no clothes on his body. Perhaps this was Chen Shicheng. However, the neighbors were too lazy to go and see, and there were no relatives to claim the body. After examination by the county officials, it was buried by the local authorities. As for the cause of death, there was no doubt. It was a common occurrence to strip clothes from a dead body, and there was no suspicion of foul play. The examination also confirmed that he had drowned while still alive, as he had clearly struggled in the water, with mud from the riverbed embedded under all ten fingernails.

June 1922.

BROTHERS

The Public Welfare Bureau has always been unable to accomplish any public service, and a few staff members are discussing personal matters in the office as usual. Qin Yitang holds a water pipe and coughs uncontrollably, causing everyone to fall silent. After a while, he lifts his flushed face, still wheezing, and says, "Yesterday, they started fighting again, from the hall all the way to the doorway. I couldn't stop them no matter how much I drank." His lips, adorned with a few gray hairs, continue to tremble. "Older brother said that the money they lost on government bonds cannot be reimbursed from public funds. They should compensate themselves..."

"You see, it's all about money," Zhang Peijun stands up generously from the broken recliner, his eyes shining with affection in their deep sockets. "I really can't understand why our own brothers have to be so petty. Isn't it all the same in the end?..."

"Where do you have brothers like yours?" Yitang says.

"We just don't care. We treat each other the same. We don't let money and wealth bother us. In doing so, there are no problems. If someone in our family demands a share, I always explain our situation to them and advise them not to be so calculating. Father is also satisfied as long as he can guide his sons..."

"But...," Yitang shakes his head.

"That's probably impossible," Wang Yuesheng says, respectfully looking at Peijun. "You truly have extraordinary brothers; I have never encountered anyone like them. You simply have no trace of selfishness or self-interest, which is not easy..."

"They fought all the way from the hall to the front gate...," Yitang says.

"Is your younger brother still busy?" Yuesheng asks.

"He's still doing eighteen hours of homework a week, plus

ninety-three essays. He's really overwhelmed. He took a few days off recently because he had a fever, probably caught a slight cold..."

"I think you should be careful," Yuesheng says solemnly. "Today's newspaper mentioned that there is an epidemic spreading..."

"What kind of epidemic?" Peijun is surprised and quickly asks.

"I can't recall clearly. It mentioned something about a fever."

Peijun strides off towards the reading room.

"It's truly rare," Yuesheng sighs with admiration as he watches him rush out. He turns to Qin Yitang and says, "Those two are like one person. If all brothers were like them, there wouldn't be any chaos in the family. I just can't learn from them..."

"They said the money lost on government bonds cannot be reimbursed from public funds..." Yitang inserts a paper coal into the pipe and says bitterly.

The temporary silence in the office is soon broken by the sound of Peijun's footsteps and the voice of the messenger. He seems to be in a state of great distress, stuttering and trembling as he speaks. He instructs the messenger to call Doctor Puteishi immediately and have him come to treat Zhang Peijun at Tongxing Apartments.

Yuesheng knows that Peijun is very worried because he knows that although Peijun trusts Western medicine, his income is not high, and he usually lives frugally. Now he has called for the first renowned and expensive doctor in this area. Yuesheng goes out to greet him and sees Peijun standing outside with a pale face, anxiously listening to the messenger making the phone call.

"What's the matter?"

"The newspaper says... says it's scar... scarlet fever. When I came to the office this afternoon, Jingfu had a bright red face... Has he already left? Please... please have them make a phone call and ask him to come immediately to Tongxing Apartments, Tongxing Apartments..."

After the messenger finishes the call, Peijun rushes into the office and grabs his hat. Yuesheng also feels anxious and follows him inside.

"When the director comes, please ask for leave for me and say that there is a sick person at home who needs to see a doctor..." Peijun nods randomly and says.

"You can go. The director may not even come," Yuesheng says.

But it seems that Peijun didn't hear him as he has already rushed out.

On the way, he no longer haggles over the fare as usual. As soon as he sees a slightly robust-looking cartman who seems capable of moving fast, he asks for the price and then steps onto the cart, saying, "Good. Just make sure to go fast!"

However, the apartment is as peaceful and quiet as usual. A young boy is still sitting outside the door playing the huqin. Peijun walks into his brother's bedroom and feels his heart pounding even harder because his face seems even redder and he is panting. He reaches out to touch his brother's forehead, which feels scorching hot.

"I don't know what illness it is. Is it serious?" Jingfu asks, his eyes filled with worried doubt, indicating that he himself also senses that something is unusual.

"It's alright, just a cold." he replied.

He was usually devoted to debunking superstitions, but at this moment, he felt that Jingfu's appearance and speech were somewhat ominous, as if the patient himself had a premonition of something. This thought made him even more uneasy, so he immediately went out and softly called the attendant, asking him to make a phone call to the hospital: Has Dr. Pu been found yet?

"Yes, yes. Not found yet," the attendant said on the phone.

Peijun not only couldn't sit still, but now he couldn't even stand still. But in his anxiety, he suddenly stumbled upon a way out: maybe it wasn't scarlet fever. However, Dr. Pu had not been found... Although Bai Wenshan, who lived in the same residence, was a traditional Chinese medicine doctor, he might be able to determine the name of the disease. However, he had said several times attacking traditional Chinese medicine, and perhaps he had already heard the request for Dr. Pu's phone call...

However, he finally went to invite Bai Wenshan.

Bai Wenshan, however, didn't mind at all. He immediately put on his tortoiseshell-framed magnifying glasses and went to Jingfu's room. He took his pulse, examined his face, and opened his shirt to look at his chest before calmly taking his leave. Peijun followed him all the way to his room.

He asked Peijun to sit down but remained silent.

"Brother Wenshan, what exactly is it...?" he couldn't help but ask.

"Scarlet fever. You see, he's already showing symptoms," Bai Wenshan replied.

"So, it's not scarlet fever?" Peijun became somewhat relieved.

"Western doctors call it scarlet fever, we Chinese medicine doctors call it scarlet rash."

This immediately made him feel cold all over.

"Can it be treated?" he asked with a worried expression.

"It can. However, it also depends on the fortune of your household."

He was already so confused that he didn't even know how he managed to ask Bai Wenshan for a prescription and leave his room. But when he passed by the telephone, he remembered that Dr. Pu had come. He still went to ask the hospital and was told that Dr. Pu had indeed been found, but he was very busy and might not be able to come until tomorrow morning. However, he emphasized that Dr. Pu must come today.

He walked into the room and turned on the light to take a look. Jingfu's face appeared even redder, with noticeable redder spots, and his eyelids were swollen. As he sat down, it felt as if he was sitting on a bed of needles. In the gradually quiet night, amid his anticipation, the whistling of every car's horn became distinctively clear to him, sometimes causing him to jump up thinking it was Dr. Pu's car coming to greet him. But before he reached the doorway, the car had already passed by; he turned back in dismay. Passing through the courtyard, he saw the bright moon had risen in the west, and the shadow of an old pagoda tree in the neighboring yard cast an even denser and gloomier atmosphere on the ground.

Suddenly, a crow cawed. It was something he often heard on

ordinary days; there were three or four crow nests on the pagoda tree. But now, he was almost startled to a stop. He walked softly into Jingfu's room, and saw him lying with closed eyes, his face seemingly swollen. He hadn't been asleep, probably heard the footsteps, and suddenly opened his eyes. Those two eyes gleamed strangely and sorrowfully in the light.

"Is it true?" Jingfu asked.

"No, no. It's me." He was surprised, somewhat flustered, and stammered, "It's me. I thought it would be better to invite a Western doctor to come and get well faster. He hasn't arrived yet..."

Jingfu didn't reply, he closed his eyes. Sitting beside the desk by the window, everything was silent, only the patient's rapid breathing and the ticking of the alarm clock could be heard. Suddenly, a car horn sounded in the distance, immediately making his heart tense. He listened as it approached, getting closer, probably reaching the entrance and about to stop, but immediately recognized that it had passed by. This happened many times, and he became familiar with the various sounds of car horns: some sounded like whistles, some like drums, some like flatulence, some like barking dogs, some like quacking ducks, some like bellowing cows, some like startled hens, some like sobbing... He suddenly resented himself: why didn't he pay attention earlier and know what Dr. Pu's car horn sounded like?

The tenants across the way had not yet returned, as usual, they were either watching a play or gathering for tea. But the night had already grown deep, and even the cars were gradually diminishing. The intense silver moonlight illuminated the paper window, making it appear white.

In the weariness of waiting, his mental and physical tension gradually relaxed, and he no longer paid attention to the car horns. But his thoughts became chaotic and took advantage of the opportunity to arise. It seemed as if he knew that Jingfu was definitely suffering from scarlet fever, and it was incurable. So how would the family finances support them, relying solely on himself? Even though they lived in a small town, the cost of living had become expensive... His own three children, his two, it was already difficult to support them, let alone send them to school. If he could only afford to send one or two to study, naturally it would be his own smart and talented child—yet everyone would surely criticize him, saying he neglected his brother's children...

What about the funeral arrangements? They didn't even have enough money to buy a coffin, how could they transport it back home? They would have to temporarily leave it at the funeral home...

Suddenly, footsteps were heard in the distance, causing him to jump up. He walked out of the room, only to realize it was the tenant from across the way.

"Xian-Diye, in the White Emperor City..."

As soon as he heard this faint and somewhat joyous chant, he felt disappointed and angry, almost wanting to go up and scold him. But then he saw the attendant carrying a lantern, the light shining on the pair of shoes behind him. In the faint glow, he could see a tall figure with a white face and a black beard. It was precisely Dr. Putisi.

As if he had found a treasure, he rushed over and led him into the patient's room. The two stood by the bedside, and he held up the lantern to illuminate.

"Doctor, he has a fever..." Peijun said breathlessly.

"When did it start?" Dr. Putisi put his hands in his trouser pockets, gazing at the patient's face, and slowly asked.

"The day before yesterday. No, the day... two days before that."

Dr. Putisi remained silent, briefly took the pulse, and then asked Peijun to hold the lantern higher so he could carefully examine the patient's face. He also asked for the covers to be lifted and the clothes to be undone for a closer look. After examining him, he extended his fingers and gently probed the patient's abdomen.

"Measles..." Dr. Putisi murmured to himself in a low voice.

"Measles?" His voice trembled with excitement.

"Measles."

"It's really measles?"

"Measles."

"You've never had measles before?"

Just as he was happily asking Jingfu, Dr. Putisi had already walked over to the desk, so he followed along. He saw Dr. Putisi place one foot on the chair, pull out a sheet of paper from the desk, and take out a short pencil from his pocket. He quickly scribbled a few illegible words on the paper. That was the prescription.

"Is the pharmacy still open?" Peijun asked as he took the prescription.

"It's fine for tomorrow. Take it tomorrow."

"Should we come for another check-up tomorrow?"

"No need for another check-up. Avoid sour, spicy, and overly salty foods. After the fever subsides, collect a urine sample and bring it to my hospital for examination. Put it in a clean glass bottle and write your name on the outside."

Dr. Putisi spoke while walking, inserting a five-yuan bill into his pocket. He went straight out. Peijun saw him off, watching him get on the car and drive away. Then he turned around and just as he entered the store, he heard two "gö gö" sounds from behind. He realized that Dr. Putisi's car horn sounded like a cow's moo. But now that he knew, it didn't matter anymore, he thought.

Inside the house, even the lights seemed pleasant. Peijun felt as if everything had been taken care of and everything around him was safe and peaceful, but his heart felt empty. He handed the money and prescription to the attendant who had come in with him, instructing him to go to Meiya Pharmacy early tomorrow morning to buy the medicine. Dr. Putisi had specifically designated that pharmacy, saying that their medications were the most reliable.

"The Meiya Pharmacy in Dongcheng! You must go there. Remember: Meiya Pharmacy!" He followed behind the attendant who was leaving, saying.

The courtyard was bathed in moonlight, shining as bright as silver. The neighbors from "In the White Emperor City" had already gone to sleep, and everything was quiet. Only the clock on the table ticked happily and evenly. Although he could hear the patient's breathing, it was soothing. He had not been sitting for long when he suddenly became happy again.

"You've grown so big, and yet you've never had measles?" He asked in amazement as if he had encountered a miracle.

"..."

"You wouldn't remember it yourself. You have to ask your mother to know."

"..."

"But Mother is not here. You've never had measles. Hahaha!"

When Pei Jun woke up in bed, the morning sun was already shining through the paper window, piercing his blurry eyes. However, he couldn't move immediately, feeling weak in his limbs and his back covered in cold sweat. He saw a child with a bleeding face standing by the bed, and he was about to hit her.

But this scene disappeared in an instant, and he was still alone sleeping in his own room, with no one else around. He untied his nightshirt to wipe away the cold sweat on his chest and back, got dressed, and headed towards Jingfu's room. He saw the neighbors from "In the White Emperor City" rinsing their mouths in the courtyard, indicating that it was already quite late.

Jingfu was also awake, lying in bed with wide-open eyes.

"How are you feeling today?" he immediately asked.

"Better... "

"Has the medicine arrived yet?"

"No."

He sat down at the desk, facing the sleeping bed; looking at Jingfu's face, it was no longer as flushed as yesterday. But his own head still felt dizzy, and fragments of the dream also flickered and emerged:

Jingfu was lying in the same position, but he was a lifeless corpse. Pei Jun was busy preparing for the burial, single-handedly carrying a coffin from outside the main gate into the hall. It seemed like they were at home, and he saw many familiar people praising him nearby...

He ordered Kang Er and his two younger siblings to go to school, but there were two children crying and clamoring to go along. The crying voices annoyed him, but at the same time, he felt a supreme authority and immense power. He saw his palm, three or four times larger than usual, as if cast in iron, slapping He Sheng's face...

Because of these haunting dream fragments, he was afraid and wanted to stand up, walk outside the room, but in the end, he didn't move. He also wanted to suppress and forget these dream fragments, but they swirled in his mind like goose feathers stirring in water, eventually surfacing:

He Sheng's face was covered in blood as he entered crying. He jumped onto the ancestral hall... Behind that child, there were a group of familiar and unfamiliar people. He knew they had all come to attack him...

"I will never lose my conscience. Don't be deceived by the child's lies..." He heard himself saying these words.

He Sheng was right beside him, and he raised his palm again...

Suddenly, he became clear-headed, feeling very tired, and there seemed to be a chill on his back. Jingfu lay quietly opposite him, breathing rapidly but evenly. The alarm clock on the table seemed to be ringing louder and louder.

He turned his body around, facing the desk. It was covered in a layer of dust. Then he turned his head to look at the paper window, where the hanging calendar had two characters written in black ink: the twenty-seventh.

The attendant came in with medicine, also carrying a package of books.

"What is it?" Jingfu opened his eyes and asked.

"Medicine." Pei Jun also woke up from his daze and replied.

"No, that package."

"Forget about it for now. Take your medicine." He gave Jingfu the medicine, then picked up the package of books and said, "It's from Suo Si. It must be the one you borrowed from him: 'Sesame and Lilies'."

Jingfu reached out to take the book, but as soon as he looked at the cover, the golden characters on the spine rubbed off, so he placed it by his pillow and quietly closed his eyes. After a while, he happily whispered:

"When I feel better, I'll translate some and send it to the Cultural Library to sell for a few coins. I wonder if they'll... "

On that day, Pei Jun arrived at the Public Welfare Bureau much later than usual, already in the afternoon. The office was filled with the smoke of Qin Yitang's water pipe. From a distance, Wang Yuesheng saw him and came to greet him.

"Ah! You're here. Is our younger brother fully recovered? I think it's not a big deal; these seasonal illnesses come every year, it's nothing to worry about. Both Yiweng and I were concerned; we kept wondering why you hadn't come yet. Now that you're here, that's great! But, look at the color of your complexion, it's quite... yes, it's quite different from yesterday."

Pei Jun also felt that this office and his colleagues were somewhat different from yesterday, unfamiliar. Although everything was still the things he was accustomed to seeing: broken clothes hooks, chipped spittoons, cluttered and dust-covered files, a broken reclining chair, Qin Yitang sitting on the chair, coughing and shaking his head while holding the water pipe...

"They've been arguing from the hall to the front door..."

"That's why," Yuesheng replied, "I said you should tell them about Brother Pei's situation and teach them to learn from him. Otherwise, they might really drive your old man to death..."

"Third Brother said that the money folded in the government bond tickets by Fifth Brother cannot be considered public funds, it should... it should..."

Yitang coughed and bent over.

"People's hearts are different..." Yuesheng said, then turned to Pei Jun, "So, nothing serious happened?"

"Nothing serious. The doctor said it's just a rash."

"A rash? Yes, now children outside are all having rashes. The three children living in my courtyard have also gotten rashes. It's nothing to worry about. But you see, yesterday you were so anxious, it was enough to move anyone who saw it. It truly embodies the phrase 'brothers harmoniously united.'"

"Did the director come to the bureau yesterday?"

"He's still 'as elusive as a yellow crane.' You can add a 'came' to the register to make it complete."

"It's said that I should compensate myself," Yitang muttered to himself. "These government bond tickets really harm people. I don't understand anything about them. As soon as you get involved, you fall for it. Yesterday, until the evening, it was still going on from the hall to the front door. Third Brother has two more children in school, and Fifth Brother also said he used public money excessively, which made him angry..."

"This is becoming even more confusing!" Yuesheng said disappointedly. "That's why, when I see you brothers, Pei Jun, I truly feel in awe. Yes, I dare say, this is not flattery to your face."

Pei Jun remained silent and saw the messenger bring in a document, so he went up to take it in his hands. Yuesheng also followed and read it while holding it, saying:

"Citizen Hao Shangshan and others submit: A nameless male corpse found dead in the eastern suburbs, requesting the sub-bureau to promptly allocate funds for coffin burial for the sake of hygiene and public welfare." I'll handle this. You should go back early, you must be concerned about your younger brother's illness. You truly are 'birds of the same feather'..."

"No!" He didn't let go. "I'll handle it."

Yuesheng stopped trying to take over. Pei Jun calmly walked to his own desk, looking at the document, and at the same time, he reached out to open the lid of the inkwell, which was covered in colorful rust spots.

November 3, 1925.

ABOUT THE AUTHOR

Lu Xun (1881-1936), originally named Zhou Shuren, was a renowned Chinese writer, thinker, and revolutionary. Considered the father of modern Chinese literature, Lu Xun played a significant role in the May Fourth Movement, a cultural and intellectual movement in China in the early 20th century. His works, including "The Diary of a Madman," "The True Story of Ah Q," and "The New Year's Sacrifice," were characterized by their realism and criticism of traditional Chinese society. Lu Xun's writings exposed the deep-rooted problems in Chinese society and called for social and cultural reforms. Through his powerful literary voice, Lu Xun became an influential figure in inspiring political and social consciousness in China. His contributions continue to resonate and influence generations of Chinese writers and intellectuals.

Printed in Great Britain
by Amazon